Adventures in the
PATAGONIAN ANDES

ROBERTO HOSNE

Adventures in the
PATAGONIAN ANDES

Translated by
Carol Duggan

CONTENTS

	FOREWORD	7
1.-	INDIAN RAIDS WERE A PROFITABLE BUSINESS	11
2.-	IN PURSUIT OF THE GREAT PURRAN	17
3.-	THE ANDES WERE THE BEST REWARD	25
4.-	"SUBLIME PASSAGE OF THE CORDILLERA"	43
5.-	THE MEDITATIONS OF CALDCLEUGH	51
6.-	A PICTURESQUE CHARACTER	55
7.-	CRAWFORD AND HIS ENGINEERS	59
8.-	SAN MARTIN IN THE HEART OF THE ANDES	65
9.-	THE PIONEERS AND THEIR CHALLENGE	71
10.-	THE EXPEDITION OF AGUSTIN DEL CASTILLO	95
11.-	FIGHTING FOR A GOOD CAUSE	103
12.-	"A GROUP OF CHOSEN MEN"	111
13.-	THE OUTLAWS	119
14.-	CONQUERING THE INVINCIBLE PEAKS	123
15.-	CELEBRATION OF MASS ON THE MOUNTAIN	129
16.-	THE PREMONITION	133
17.-	"ANDINISM": LEGENDS AND TECHNIQUE	139
18.-	ICE CATHEDRALS	143
19.-	THE TORRE: THE MOST DIFFICULT PEAK	147
20.-	A LAND OF LEGEND	157
21.-	A CONTROVERSIAL JOURNEY	163
	REFERENCES	167

FOREWORD

All those travelers who crossed the Andes tried, each in his own way, to transmit the sensations they felt when faced with the overpowering, grandiose presence of this huge stone mass. They were also aware that no words could even come close to defining that which seemed to exceed human dimensions.

The general idea was that "it was on too large a scale to be grasped by human imagination". Darwin, after his travels all over the world, said that Patagonia was still a vivid memory in his mind, and that he would never forget the overwhelming vision that dazzled him from the snowcapped peaks of the Andes. Haigh was of the opinion that any man facing the andean mountain range "becomes conscious of his own insignificance".

Many episodes took place in these surroundings. Some of them involved local characters, such as the stories about natives who used secret mountain passes to smuggle animals they stole in the *pampas;* in a way, they were the originators of a type of transgression that finally became a generally accepted form of trade.

Other chronicles refer to important events that took place while this country was fighting for its independence. The *Criollos* managed to free themselves from Spanish dominion thanks to the epic performance of San Martín and his army, who were able to get across the steep, dangerous passes of the *Cordillera* and defeated the powerful royalist forces. The impressions of European travelers –mainly Englishmen- also manage to convey another aspect of San Martín´s personality; they saw him as a man eager to promote the Enlightenment and the spreading of progressive ideas. Sizing him from a strictly military angle, Caldcleugh remarked: "His crossing the Andes is usually compared to Napoleon´s feat when crossing Mt. Saint Bernard. However, considering the advantages Napoleon could count in his favor –e.g. a disciplined army and an abundance of supplies and reinforcements-, it is obvious that San Martín´s achievement is even more admirable".

Proctor praised the liberal ideas and "San Martín´s patronage…to silence the clamor of the enemies of progress"; he revealed how "San Martín frequently came to our meetings; he always amused us with interesting anecdotes. He was a remarkable story-teller, captivating his audience with his expressive face and his eloquence…".

England – which was in those days the world´s most powerful empire-, considered the Andes could be a tempting possibility for those feverish capitalists who operated in the Stock Market and were always on the look-out for profitable investments; they even sent experts to discover mineral deposits on both sides of the Andean range. On their return, many of them described their experiences in stories full of amusing anecdotes and comments that revealed acute powers of observation.

Of course, many of those who read these books were yearning for adventure and all too keen to launch into some extravagant voyage across the ocean, eager to climb the mountains and decipher their secrets. Fiction and legend were a powerful mix in the many incursions carried out by intrepid adventure-lovers who always balanced on the dangerous edge of experience.

These expeditions were always dramatic; after leaving Buenos Aires they had to undertake an endless, monotonous voyage across never-ending, uninhabited plains, "…a thousand miles of what could be the least interesting country in the world…" and spend the night in miserable stations reeking with the smell of burnt cinders. The only thing that kept them alive and hopeful was the anticipation of experiencing the "sublime crossing of the cordillera".

Then came the pioneers: fearless, hard-working people who settled at the foot of the mountains in absolute solitude.

Some years later, the need to examine the topography of the land, and then the definition of the borders with Chile assembled explorers, geographers and naturalists. These, together with the pioneers and the few survivors of practically extinct aboriginal tribes, were the core of society in southern Patagonia. Which is, of course, an eloquent example of a loneliness and solitude hardly conceivable in any other part of the country.

The pioneers were very often victims of political intrigue. When it came to a topic of vital importance such as the distribution of land, they were frequently pushed aside and some influential "friend or associate" became beneficiary of what was really their due. Fortunately, they were well represented by Andreas Madsen: "I turned back, only a few steps. But then I took a firm stand to fight with my back against the wall (the wall was the Fitz Roy peak)".

The Andean mountain range exerts an enormous power of attraction over a legion of mountain-climbers who are willing to risk their lives in order to dare its impregnable vertical stone walls. In some cases, the outcome was success, in others, failure. But all these ventures were in keeping with the magnificence of the surrounding scene. Casimiro Ferrari, the leading exponent of mountain-climbers who settled in Los Glaciares several years ago until his death in August 2001, once admitted that work allowed him to live, but mountaineering and Patagonia made him feel alive.

The vast Andean territory has hosted many adventures where human experience has lingered on the edge of greatness.

During almost five hundred years this vast territory has attracted all kinds of people, each pursuing his own particular dream, all willing to pay the price to keep the fire of their illusions burning.

This is a history made of strong passions: greed, lust for gold or power, the ambition to discover and to conquer, the will to overcome difficulties, the challenge behind scientific quests, the courage to explore and face unknown circumstances, the daily act of faith when a man´s life and values are at stake.

Roberto Hosne

1.- INDIAN RAIDS WERE A PROFITABLE BUSINESS

"...it's like trying to hold down a river".

Indian raids were called *malocas* or *malones*. These were, in fact, devastating onslaughts carried out -mostly by *Araucanos*- on the *estancias* of Buenos Aires, Córdoba and Mendoza, with the sole purpose of stealing horses and cattle. Quite different, of course, to the battles that certain tribes fought as part of the war against the Spanish conqueror. There was nothing epic about these raids. People were terrified of the *maloqueros* who were violent and cruel; they not only stole animals but also kidnapped women and children and destroyed everything that came their way.

In order to sell the stolen goods, the *Araucanos* knew many secret passes which allowed them to cross the animals into Chile. All through the XVIII century traffic across the Andean mountain range was very intense, in spite of the efforts of certain army officers who wanted to put a stop to this type of trade. The Chilean general Thomas O'Higgins did everything in his power to try to force the Indian chieftains to stop this illegal traffic, but the answer he got was "...it's like trying to hold down a river".

The *maloca* was a carefully planned financial operation which, after the commercial transaction in Chile, allowed the tribe to go back to their usual occupations: the *cacique* returned with enough wealth and prestige to pursue his political ambitions and aspire to becoming an *Ulmen* or *Cacique Gobernador*. The other Indians could go back to their activities, or gang up with other natives, or join the *Araucano* army as warriors.

The *Huiliches* (from the South) were the most inclined to cattle robbery; they were brave warriors and were trained in a very strict army-like discipline; complete submission towards their leader and a lethal talent for war were basic characteristics of this tribe that systematically stole cattle from the *Hispano-Criollos*.

Around 1550 the Spanish conquerors disembarked horses in Valdivia. These rapidly expanded throughout all Araucania. Even though they were, at the time, exotic animals, they were rapidly assimilated by the Indians as part of their culture and traditions. In no time they became expert riders and learnt to train the

11

horses to become fast runners.

In those days it was not uncommon for Indians to herd several thousand head of cattle while carrying terrified women on their horses on those long journeys, along dangerous and secluded mountain passes into Chile. Sometimes the passes were so steep it was practically impossible to see the sky above. Which of course must have increased the fear in these women who were strapped to the horses and brutally held down by fierce savages who "smelt of skunk" (they used to soak their spears in urine). The victims were revolted by their filthy breath which, together with the howls and piercing screams and the disagreeable smell of ostrich grease they smeared on their bodies were a preview of the kind of life and treatment they had in store.

The Indians were intent on stealing and, if possible, tried to avoid killing. They only took greater risks when they suspected there were young women hiding inside a house. And if they actually did find any, they seized the unfortunate girls and dragged them away to the Indian camp; the young, attractive prisoners were kept apart for the *caciques*; those not so young, or unattractive, were subjected by whoever fancied them, and forced to hard labor; they had to put up with abuse, not only from the men but also from the jealous Indian women who enjoyed beating them on the sly. And all this they accepted without complaining,

The *estancias* confronted a very serious problem when the *cimarrón* cattle (unclaimed cattle that roamed the pampas) were slaughtered to extinction by Indians and white cattlemen: the *maloqueros* needed cattle both for their own consumption and to supply their clients on the other side of the Andes, so they resorted to raiding the ranches and obtaining the necessary merchandise by force.

That´s the reason why the *maloca* became a regular commercial activity, which was practically monopolized by the *Araucanos*.

Going back as far as mid XVII century, there was a Dutch military settlement in Valdivia that depended on the Indians for cattle supply. When the natives didn´t have the amount of animals requested they asked for a period of time – usually a few months- to assemble and deliver the goods. Then they crossed the *cordillera* and organized raids to round up the animals they needed for their personal use and to meet their commercial agreements in Chile.

In 1780, the pilot Basilio Villarino informed Francisco de Viedma that some three thousand Indians had been seen near Choele Choel herding approximately eighty thousand head of cattle. They came from Buenos Aires and were bound for Valdivia. Villarino also mentioned that the natives took six captive women with them. Félix de Azara was convinced that "…the indians stole cattle in Buenos Aires to cross them into Chile".

Viceroy Vértiz accused the Chilean authorities of being too lenient with these predatory practices and demanded they put a stop to such abusive policies.

Throughout history the *Araucanos* have earned their reputation as warriors. The historian Tomás Guevara also described other character traits typical of this tribe, such as: "…he lacks foresight; that is because he is limited both in memory and in the ability to associate and generalize ideas; he lacks the possibility of deducing from past and present facts that which will happen in the future. That explains why, when he sells his animals and grain, he doesn´t take the precaution of keeping enough provisions for the rest of the year, or why he consumes all these goods at once, in a family party or religious ceremony (…) His inclination to steal originates in the incapacity to distinguish between good and evil".

The *Araucano* was used to resisting hunger, thirst and bad weather during his travels. "…he can resist the freezing cold, rain or extreme heat without effort. He can be seen crossing the cordillera barefoot in midwinter, or getting wet during a storm, wearing only a thin vest while his rug is neatly tucked away under the saddle."

The Chilean authorities were very particular about controlling the exchange of liquor and wine…and iron instruments. The Bishop of Concepción, in 1784, was shocked by the way "these enemies are supplied with weapons and the facilities given to them to raise horses and manufacture lances and *machetes* or sabers". He added that all these things caused "countless sins" and that it was impossible to "gain anything with these indians, neither with the State nor with Religion".

The *Araucanos* then started to buy weapons at bargain prices from Spanish arms dealers who operated near the border, in a kind of promiscuous community where fugitives, deserters and "white *maloqueros*" coexisted with *gauchos* and half-castes, settlers, soldiers, indian servants and lancers, criminals, herdsmen and farmers. Violence and crime were routine in this heterogeneous group of barbarians and outsiders who didn´t respect any law: neither the royalist laws nor those established in the ancient aboriginal traditions. This was a no-man´s-land with a majority of inhabitants who lacked the minimum scruples or social codes.

In vain, Governor Guill y Gonzaga tried to pursue them with the intention of having them punished: they were experts at hiding in the secret passes of the cordillera and getting away.

The white *maloqueros* were the most violent of the bunch, to the extent that they even lost the natives's support when these converted to the Christian faith.

Little by little, the border became the meeting place of all kinds of criminals: ferocious rural outlaws, ex-soldiers, *gauchos* who were very deft in the use of knives and lassoes, corrupt Indian chiefs who fancied fashionable hats, velvet stockings and stirrups made of silver, drunken *conas* who took the captive women from Buenos Aires as wives while the white cattle thief practiced polygamy among the indians...

The natives generally had a weakness for silver stirrups. Specially the *Toqui* tribe. And apparently, they were the cause of an incident that involved the famous chief Calfucurá. It all happened during a party given in his honor, in Manquehue: it was a real feast, with lambs and beef roasting next to a huge crackling fire and large quantities of *chicha* being passed around, when suddenly they were attacked by a group of *Mapuches* from Boroa.

That episode formed part of the oral tradition of the *Araucanos*, the details of which were transmitted by Alberto Huichulef to the Chilean journalist Mayo Calvo: "...the people of Manquehue were unable to defend themselves and would all have been killed by the *maloqueadores* if it hadn´t been for Calfucurá who took control of the situation (...) The people of Boroa crossed the cordillera to raid and steal in Argentina, and later returned carrying with them the cattle, the women and children they had stolen. But they had to pass through Llaima, precisely the place where the people of Manquehue had, out of gratitude, invited Calfucurá to stay; and he pounced on them and stripped them of the booty".

In Boroa they had no intention of letting that incident pass and they started to plan a revenge. Their purpose was to recover the cattle and prisoners and, what was even more important, to kill Calfucurá; word got round to him that the people of Boroa and their allies were planning to attack him, and he decided to ask Chief Truf-Truf for help. On his visit to *Cacique* Truf-Truf, Calfucurá laid at his feet the two silver stirrups he had taken as a gift.

Chief Truf-Truf bent down, took the stirrups and threw them away, saying: *"I am not going to lose my people for these silver stirrups. I do not intend to lose my people, to have them killed for these tokens. No".*

Faced with the impending onslaught, Calfucurá went to Santiago and asked the army for help. They promised to send some soldiers on the condition that he returned the favor providing them with women.

Alberto Huichulef also commented that Calfucurá (his name meant "blue stone") was a man who had great authority over his men and was ferocious when commanding a raid. He was a proud and cruel man and believed he descended from lions; he killed all those who opposed him, very often with his own hands. He had twenty-five women or, as he put it, "twenty-five fires". Obviously, he left many descendants in the district.

The fearful Boroans were finally defeated and returned to their Indian camps. According to data given to Mayo Calvo by the *Cacique* Rosamel Antimilla, missions with priests and nuns of different congregations had settled in those indian camps. And, whenever the missionaries needed to buy food and provisions they went on voyages that could last three or four months.

A group of missionaries once went on one of those trips leaving thirty nuns behind. To their horror, the following day the convent was raided. "And that explains why –says Antimilla- in Boroa there are *Mapuches* with pale blue eyes. They turned out very *simpáticos* these *mapuches*, they look like *gringos*. The *caciques* also took some of those nuns to Choshuenco, and there are plenty of blue-eyed *mapuches* down there too. And when the *padrecitos* (the priests) returned they found nobody. So they said: "the nuns are women, just like any other woman. The *caciques* have taken them "just let it be", and that´s why the *Mapuches* after the raid were born fair".

Rosamel Antimilla said his father had told him that story and that he, in turn, got it from his family. And now his children, present here, will later tell it to their grandchildren.

Both the Argentine and Chilean *Mapuches* used to cross the Andes frequently because they had family and folks on either side of the border, and it was customary to go visiting when there was some special festivity or celebration.

When Calfucurá died his son, Namuncurá, inherited eight leagues in Azul, in the province of Buenos Aires, land which had originally been given to them by the Argentine government. Namuncurá, together with other *caciques*, went to Government House with the idea -according to Huichulef-, of negotiating with President Roca the return of those lands to them, their rightful owners.

During the meeting Roca offered cigars to all of them and then he approached Namuncurá and said to him:

"¿You are Namuncurá?"

He answered affirmatively and the president repeated the same question three more times. The fourth time he said:

> *"You have caused the government here great damage. You have killed many soldiers and now I have the right to take you to the plaza and shoot four bullets into you".*

The Indian chief didn´t budge. He looked stonily at Roca, pretending to be totally impassive in front of this man that seemed to him a sort of "bull".

> *"Well, I forgive you because you´re an ignorant being. Had you been a civilized being you would certainly not get away with this. The lands the government gave your father have already been sold. You have nothing, so just look for another place and, when you find it, you can settle".*

Huichulef tells that Namuncurá settled in Junín, next to the river San Ignacio, and that way he was able to have his own land.

Clemente Onelli collaborated with Perito Moreno in the Limits Committee in charge of the demarcation of the Argentine-Chilean border. During one of his expeditions he approached the location where Namuncurá lived with his folks: "…when nothing was left of the warrior tribes of brave Cacique Namuncurá (stone foot) and they led a peaceful existence as shepherds, the past glories have remained in the past and are only remembered every now and then on libation days. I spent a few moments with the old battle fighter of the Pampas; he, together with his family and his folks, they all had a look of animal submission on their faces, the look of a beast that has been tamed".

Some time later Huichulef happened to meet Namuncurá in Junín de los Andes and stopped to have a chat. The chief of police was looking on and made fun of Namuncurá who had difficulty in speaking Spanish. The *Mapuche* chief murmured to Huichulef:

> *"I have been a much feared chief. Just my name being mentioned and everybody trembled. And now I see that anybody can mock me…"*

But he was not the only Indian chief who had to put up with mockery. The great Purrán was also dishonored and even spent eight long years in prison, on the island Martín García.

2.- IN PURSUIT OF THE GREAT PURRAN

Some local scouts discovered fresh trails left by *maloqueros* and they immediately advised the army regiment. A commission of 47 men of the 11th. Cavalry Regiment was organized under Major Manuel Ruybal´s command and went in their pursuit.

"We followed the trails marked by the guides –reported Guillermo Pechmann, a young officer who was narrator of this incursion- and our sly, tireless chief only stopped for a very few moments during the whole day to give the horses some rest".

On the following day they found other traces such as still burning cinders of a recent fire and tracks made by cows, goats and horses that went straight in the direction of the *cordillera*. In spite of Major Ruybal´s impatience, he was forced to halt and let his soldiers eat and rest for a while.

They took all sorts of precautions. Sentries were appointed in strategic places, and other soldiers made a thorough reconnaissance of the site. Then they carefully lit a fire. They rested that night and left at dawn. After traveling for quite a few hours, in the afternoon, they heard some dogs barking, which led them to believe that they were already very close to the *maloqueros* and that they would most likely catch up with them and their herd the next morning. They crossed the *cordillera* by Los Barros.

Officer Pechmann was deeply touched by the experience of crossing the *cordillera* for the first time, as a soldier of the 11th Cavalry Regiment, in 1880. He was still a vigorous youth who embraced his new life in the army with fervent enthusiasm. He often felt both surprised and bewildered when confronted with certain facts of the military routine, and he was conscious that his reactions were not always in keeping with what was expected of him in his new role.

He was deeply impressed by a discussion he once witnessed between two officers. One of the officers was called Molina, and the other´s name was Alegre. Apparently Alegre had imposed a penalty on Molina who, in turn, promised that when he left the glasshouse he would kick his ass. Alegre (who, according to Pechmann, was always throwing his weight around and putting on airs of straight-

17

soldier-decent-guy-) immediately set him free and said the reason for doing so was to give him the opportunity of keeping his promise (that is, to kick him). Molina was described by Pechmann as "very dark. What's worse he was unclean, and dressed in a slovenly, untidy fashion. He was a Second Lieutenant on commission. He could be clean, although he was less of a show-off than Alegre").

When Alegre set Molina free he told him they would meet at one-thirty outside the barracks so he could keep his promise. Both men met punctually and walked away about one kilometer. Molina was armed with a saber and Alegre with the arc of a crossbow (which had an iron core to make beatings more painful) that was generally used to punish the recruits. He also used a rug to protect his arm from the saber thrusts. Later on, in the barracks, Pechmann found out that if he hadn't been present witnessing the duel, Alegre would have got hold of a dagger he always kept hidden and would have "cut" Molina up. In any case, Molina received so many blows to his head that he was unable to put on his cap; he also had so many "bleeding bumps and bruises on his face and hands" that Pechmann had to take him to a pond nearby for him to wash. In the meantime, Alegre kept badgering him, urging him on so that he might "finish him off".

Two months later, when he was out riding with a group of soldiers, Pechmann saw some condors overhead. Sergeant Teófilo Gaitán remarked:

"That means news…"

And, in fact, they found nine dead bodies lying next to a mound of saltpeter. It was a horrifying scene: all naked and mutilated, heads severed from the bodies, guts strewn on the ground… Gaitán carefully walked among the dead bodies, studying the scene with a knowing look. He said:

"they're Chileans and the Indians took them by surprise. They must have killed them yesterday, not before, because they don't stink. By the look of the trails there must be about twenty-five Indians bound South".

At the fort they were told the victims were Chileans who were going towards the salt mounds to load their Remingtons.

That was Pechmann's first encounter with a killing.

They finally reached the mountain range, and started out on the dangerous crossing: riding through narrow passes and between high, craggy stone walls, marching at a snail's pace along steep paths. They waded across streams of turbulent waters and went through valleys and deep ravines. They stopped every now and then for a short rest, looking forward to the special break they had planned for the evening. They were even going to slaughter a mare.

Just when they were about to indulge in some delicious pieces of meat the sentry sent word that a party of Indians was seen prowling in the neighborhood; obviously upset at this untimely interruption, a sergeant and some men went after the *maloqueros*, who escaped leaving their spears behind. A couple of Indians who were riding on mules had dismounted and continued on foot; there was no doubt that the drove was nearby and that they would come face-to-face with the Indians in no time.

The inevitable encounter with the *Mapuches* made them very uneasy. The veteran soldiers were of the opinion that the *Araucanos* were fierce thieves but very courageous fighters, quite the opposite to the *Pampas* who were just as cruel when looting but were otherwise cowards.

Shortly after setting out in pursuit of the Indians they found the fresh trail. Major Ruybal distributed several groups of soldiers in a row while keeping an eye on the Indians who parleyed on the opposite bank of the river Bío Bío. When the *maloqueros* realized they'd been discovered they ran away leaving plenty of animals behind, much to the satisfaction of the soldiers who knew their rations were assured.

Through a local villager, a chilean called Domingo Cabeza, Major Ruybal managed to communicate with the *Cacique* who was no other than the famous Purrán. The message he sent was that this was an advance party of an army that was in the rear, and that they were not out for warfare but to draw up a peace treaty for which he had been authorized by the Argentine government. Purrán replied that he didn't want to fight either, he was all for living in peace and being on good terms with the Argentine government.

Then came the stage of preliminary negotiations. Both Purrán and Major Ruybal sent their respective emissaries. Whenever Purrán sent one of his men across the river, Ruybal sent back some mares as a gift. They agreed that Purrán would go in the afternoon to sign the treaty but he didn't show up then nor the next day as promised. At first he excused himself on the grounds that there was danger of the Bío Bío overflowing. But later he didn't even offer an excuse. At each crossing, his emissaries just said that the meeting was postponed for the following morning or afternoon and they returned with the gifts (mares). Until Ruybal ran out of mares.

Then he sent an ultimatum. "You go tell General Purrán that it´s been three days now that he´s been deceiving me with the promise that he'll come to talk with me, and I must return. So, if the General doesn´t come here today to embrace and sign the agreement, I will be forced to believe that he´s acting in bad faith and will be obliged to cross over with my troops and fight with him because those are my orders".

Another of Purrán´s messengers crossed over some time later to say the *Cacique* would come that same afternoon, but that Ruybal´s men had to retreat and that only he was to meet Purrán and his interpreters.

Major Ruybal asked his troops (except for ten soldiers and the bugler) to camp about one hundred and fifty meters away, under a cluster of trees beside the river, where they could be seen by the Indians from the opposite river bank. He told his soldiers to take meat for a good *asado*, and kettles, *mates, yerba*, sugar and whatever liquor was left. Then they had to get a big fire crackling and improvise many seats around it.

He made the ten soldiers and the bugler hide with their rifles loaded, some sixty meters from where the parley was to be held. The bugler had to keep his eyes focused on the Major with the bugle ready for action. He warned them: "I will sit down with the Indians; just a few moments after that I'll take off my hat with my left hand and will wipe my brow with my right hand complaining about the heat. At that moment the bugler will sound the reveille. That is a signal indicating you must charge against the *Araucanos*, killing as many as you can, except for Chief Purrán who must be kept alive at any cost; he'll be sitting on my right".

The remaining soldiers had to wait at one hundred and fifty meters distance, mounted and ready to charge at the sound of the bugle.

Purrán and twenty-five Indians armed with spears crossed the river at three in the afternoon. Around eight hundred Indian warriors stayed behind. Pechmann noted that they crossed swiftly in a big raft, and then "...Purrán, chief of the Pehuenches and Picunches, known as ruler of the Andes, disembarked."

The Major greeted him with the customary ceremonial procedures and both men shook hands. They all sat down in a circle round the fire and *mate* was passed around. Officer Ferreyra spoke the *Araucano* language and acted as interpreter. He translated Major Ruybal´s message to Purrán, who hardly knew any Spanish. Some high-ranking members of the tribe kept away from the group. They stood against some trees in the background and kept close watch on the goings-on between both parties.

When Purrán was blamed for the excesses committed by his people he firmly denied the charges; he said it was a long time since his people had abandoned the *maloquero* practices, and that "if there had been some countrymen involved in a raid it must have been Namuncurá o Queupo´s people with whom he had nothing to do". (The truth is, Purrán cunningly avoided taking an active part in the raids, but the *maloquero* chiefs knew that he was a firm buyer of stolen cattle which he then fattened on his own lands. It was calculated that he sold an average of thirty thousand head of cattle a year to the Chileans and that Domingo Cabeza, who was an occasional go-between, had a leasing arrangement with Purrán).

Then the other Indians approached the group and took part in the conversation. Officer Ferreyra was most impressed with their speech, with arguments he found hard to disprove. And he said as much to Major Ruybal.

In Pechmannn´s opinion: "Our chief must have felt somewhat nervous at having such an important prey at his side because he completely forgot about the pre-arranged signal and, when only fifteen minutes had gone by, or due to lack of foresight, he took off his hat. The bugler mistook that gesture for a cue and promptly sounded the reveille". The crouching soldiers left their hiding place and began shooting while the others fanned out on the river bank and opened fire on the indians on the opposite side.

Some indignant chiefs and Purrán himself began to wave their *boleadoras*; other indians ran as fast as they could to avoid getting shot by the soldiers pursuing them; and there was still another group who tried to escape getting into the river, but most of these drowned.

Purrán seemed determined to fight to the very end with his *boleadoras*, which he swung violently around while he insulted the Major and the soldiers that surrounded him. He actually managed to hit Corporal Baigorria who, in an attack of fury and aided by a soldier, knocked the *cacique* down.

While the soldier rested the point of his bayonet on Purrán´s chest the other men pinioned his arms to the ground.

He rose and fixed on them a look of hatred and contempt. Then he addressed Ruybal: "Well, you no kill my people". The major ordered cease-fire although it was already too late for that. Purrán looked around him and saw that all his companions were dead.

"Then –continues Pechmann- Sergeant Saturnino González appeared with rugs and braces and showed them to the major. He explained these belonged to an Indian whom he shot because he refused to give himself up. The Major asked Purrán if he knew who these articles belonged to. The chief sadly answered: "yes, they belonged to my brother". "Oh, dear! –said the major- well now, Purrán, you must learn to forgive because these are the consequences of war…""

Sergeant González had chased Purrán´s brother "…along the river bank, and when he caught up with him -according to his own confession- he was careful not to pierce the rugs. With one hand he lifted them and with the other he repeatedly dug the knife into his body".

Pechmann, who actually saw the dead body, confirmed that it was "…riddled with terrible knife wounds. The sergeant could have taken him prisoner instead of killing him. But he was well-known for being a bloodthirsty man…he used to say he served under Rosas".

One hour later the raft returned with one hundred and fifty spears and a large amount of garments and woven stuff. "…those few wounded men who returned were killed, but there were certainly more wounded among those who managed to escape".

The Major urged his troops to show "…the utmost respect and consideration for the *Cacique*".

Purrán was the sole survivor of the committee that crossed the river to sign a peace treaty.

At the sound of reveille, an Indian who suspected an ambush had stealthily approached the Major. He thrust his knife at him, but failed in his attempt to wound Ruybal. When he realized the only damage done was to Ruybal´s clothes the native started to swear and insult the major in a fit of rage. Then he tried to escape towards the river. He was seen by Officer Ferreyra, who didn´t have the courage to kill him. It was only when the *Araucano* was diving into the river that Sergeant Clemente Zapata finished him off with a clean shot.

"Thousands of cows, eight hundred fat oxen, mares, a large number of beautiful horses, dairy cows, goats and thousands of sheep" were then sold to the cattle dealers and the money was distributed by the chief of the Border Police, Commander Ortega, to the chiefs, officers and troopers who took part in "the battle against the spears of Chief Purrán". That figures in the report.

Purrán was taken first to Buenos Aires and then to Martín García, where he remained a prisoner for eight years. A prominent citizen promised to set him free, on condition that Purrán point out the exact spot where he assured having seen a silver mine. The *Araucano* chief accepted this proposal and mentioned a site called Ranquilón, in Neuquén; it was rumored that all this was a hoax, that Purrán invented all this on the chance that someone would buy the story and, tempted by the idea of owning a silver mine, would get him out of jail. That would give him time to plan his escape.

So they set out on their journey towards the mine. That night they stopped to rest in Chos Malal and, before dawn, somebody arranged Purran´s escape.

Actually, one of the soldiers suspected something was up because that evening, when they were all sitting around the fire having *mate*, he thought he caught a glimpse of a *chasque* galloping at a distance. He wondered if it couldn´t be a messenger that had to give the order to set Purrán free...

And so, two days later Purrán crossed the Andes by a secret pass and rode on horseback all the way to La Araucaria. Of course, he´d lost a lot of his previous arrogance and style.

He lived there till the end of his days.

This takes us to the subject of the *chasques* (native couriers). The Indians submitted some of their chosen youths to a very strict training process which could last several years. It usually began during puberty and carried on until they were considered fit to become messengers for the tribe. Their task was a risky one, sometimes they had to ride for days crossing deserts or mountains just to take messages between tribes, or to call a raid or arrange a parley.

They rode tirelessly for days on end, racing across the desert to fulfill their mission on time. Nothing daunted them, neither the distance nor the blazing sun or the freezing cold.

But all that belongs to the past. The voyages across dangerous terrain, the huge distances that were covered in the name of ideals and beliefs, all that belongs to the realm of legends. The same goes for the *chasques*. After the breakdown of the Indian empires, these legendary characters became a part of history.

3.- THE ANDES WERE THE BEST REWARD

"We could never have imagined the marvels our eyes beheld..."

An Englishman called John Miers disembarked in Buenos Aires in 1819, just passing through on his way to Chile. At the age of 25 he was already well-known for his research in chemistry, more specifically, for his investigations in the composition of nitrogen. Owing to his perseverance in all his activities, and his acute powers of observation, he would undoubtedly have become a renowned scientist in his country.

But one day chance got in the way of his carefully planned existence and his life underwent a complete change. Lord Cochrane, who was at the time living in Chile, made Miers an offer he couldn't refuse: "...together with a friend we have assembled considerable capital to launch our new enterprise. Our intention was to install, in Chile, an industry to refine, roll out and process the copper used for linings. As far as we knew, we had a promising future before us, and the almost complete certainty that we could make a fortune..."

Tomas Cochrane was a Scotsman. He was both an army and a naval officer. Born in 1775, he was the 10th Count of Dundonald and grandson of a naval commander. He started his life at sea at the age of 18, under the orders of an uncle. He was promoted to captain at the age of 25, and carried out several actions which were evidence of his daring and courageous character. Nevertheless, many of the techniques he used in battle were against the rules and actually shocked his superiors. For instance, in order to surprise and attack his enemies he once flew a Danish flag and pretended his ship was in quarantine. He also used the mistaken-identity trick on the Spaniards by hoisting a North American flag. He deceived them and then promptly boarded a frigate. And when he encountered a powerful French fleet, he showed an almost suicidal audacity.

Nobody doubted his courage. But among his opponents he had many enemies who would have been only too glad to witness an abrupt end to his career. His downfall came about eventually, not through disciplinary measures taken by the Admiralty but by some shady financial affair. In 1814 somebody called Du Bourg announced that Napoleon had been defeated. Cochrane promptly made a very profitable operation selling shares at several points above their value. It was soon discovered that Du Bourg had been in touch with Cochrane and that the information he gave was false. Cochrane was sentenced to one year in prison and obliged to pay a fine of 1000 pounds. He was expelled from the Navy and from Parliament.

When he had served his sentence he went to Chile with his wife and five-year-old son. There he joined the Navy and commanded the fleet that fought for independence against Spain, showing his famed courage and expertise in several victorious battles.

He was a very brave soldier and also a shrewd businessman, and it was this part of his personality that drove him to get in touch with Miers and lure him to these far-off regions. Miers, on his part, had married recently, and both he and his young wife (who was pregnant) were keen on accepting Cochrane´s offer. After all, -they reasoned- obtaining a good financial position at the age of thirty justified postponing scientific research for a time.

That decided Miers to travel to Buenos Aires. From there he parted on a long, tiresome and hazardous journey to Chile, during which he wrote his impressions in notes which he later compiled in the book "Viajes por Chile y el Plata". Many people were annoyed by the intolerance and contempt he expressed in his notes. Certain members of the Argentine society were quite shocked by his opinions, which they considered offensive towards prominent citizens of the local aristocracy.

Shortly after reaching the *cordillera*, Miers´s wife lived through an episode that became a part of the regional folklore of stories and adventures that circulated in the style of oral tradition. All along the andean range, everybody knew what had happened to Miers´s wife. Even famous travelers like Captain Francis Bond Head, Robert Proctor and Peter Schmidtmeyer, told her story, took notes and made comments…

Bond Head wrote: "…an English lady arrived together with a seven-year-old boy, two or three younger children and some *peones*. With no other protection they had crossed the Cordillera and rode some fourteen hours on horseback until they reached Uspallata… The eldest son, a very handsome lad, had ridden all the way, but the smaller chubby-cheeked children were carried by the *peones*, on pillows placed on their horses. At the Villavicencio station I overheard that, in spite of the situation in the desert and the general lack of comfort, an Englishwoman who was crossing to Chile with her husband (John Miers) some seven years back, had remained there until both she and her small child could face the dangerous journey. When I saw the miserable lodgings that had been her home during that time, I thought to myself "What a rough time she must have gone through!". The lady that was now bound for Uspallata was no other than Mrs. Miers, whose sufferings I have described, and the handsome lad was her son, who was born in Villavicencio. He´d been in Chile since then, and now this grownup boy had crossed the *cordillera* and was about to show his little brothers the primitive *rancho* where he was born".

After an exhausting and risky journey from Buenos Aires, the Miers reached Mendoza at midday on the 25ᵗʰ of April, 1819. They stayed at a roadside inn, in a murky little room with no window, which meant that if they wanted light they had to open the door that gave onto the yard.

It was Sunday. At night, after dinner, they went to a kind of drawing-room where there were many people gathered around the tables, playing *monte*. Miers describes the scene:

"Each table was covered with heaps of money, several stacks of gold coins, others of pesos... I was astonished at the size of the wagers and the large amount of money on the tables. The games succeeded one another with surprising speed and an anxious expectancy was shared by players and lookers-on alike".

The fact that the arrival of "two strangers" –he and his wife- had passed quite unnoticed annoyed Miers, specially because "...the presence of an English lady should have aroused some curiosity. But then, except for some very few exceptions, this is characteristic in all South America". Of course he exaggerated, but that was the way he usually reacted when faced with unpleasant situations: he felt compelled to improvise some generalized definition.

He was even more surprised when he saw the men suddenly making a dash for the door, colliding with each other, elbowing their way through, making hasty signs of the cross and trying desperately to leave the room. Some fell on their knees, others beat their breasts while murmuring the Our Father, or raised their arms towards heaven pleading for mercy...or indulgence.

The English couple watched the scene dumbfounded. After a brief, silent pause, all the men rushed back to their previous places and continued playing.

The panic was caused by an earth tremor, "...a slight earthquake to which we –as strangers- were still insensitive, because neither of us felt the least sensation".

They went out for a walk and suddenly came upon "...a ceremony of one of the convents, but I couldn´t find out what it was about". A procession of monks, each one carrying a lantern with a burning candle, slowly walking, "chanting and singing psalms". The silver crosses and chalices shone in the darkness.

The following morning he woke up feeling drowsy and in a bad mood. He complained of having suffered the most terrible torture: hundreds of filthy bedbugs (*chinches*) attacked him, leaving large, painful swellings on his skin. He couldn´t sleep: "...I was forced to get dressed and sit on a chair, that way I was able to rest awhile..." And so on, until he decided to begin the routine he had planned for that day, one of them being the meeting with Governor Luzuriaga to see about their passports. He showed up at 10 a.m. but was told that the Governor hadn´t got out of bed yet so he was requested to return at midday.

He returned to the inn, much to his wife´s relief who could then get rid of "a new friend –the inn-keeper´s wife- who did nothing but prattle about clothes". This same woman later approached their room, bearing an invitation from Governor Luzuriaga´s wife to a social gathering. One of the invited guests was General San Martín. She suggested that it would be a fine gesture if Mrs. Miers sold the clothes she had prepared for her baby to Mrs. Luzuriaga. Or, better still, to give them to her as a gift. Mrs. Miers was reluctant to part with the clothes because she was now very near childbirth, but she agreed to lend the patterns, if necessary. The inn-keeper´s wife soon returned with another message from Mrs. Luzuriaga, expressing her regret for having to postpone the gathering.

Miers made acquaintance with two physicians: Doctor Colesberry, a North American, and a Scotsman, Doctor Gillies. Funnily enough, they were both living in Mendoza for health reasons. They were full of praise for the climate in Cuyo which, they considered, had cured their lung problems. And they both agreed that the people in that region were very healthy.

John Miers was inclined to agree with them, although he had seen many cases of goiter. But he admitted it wasn´t "combined with cretinism, which is usually found in some alpine districts. I didn´t see any idiots either, nor cases of mental derangement. Deformity is rare and the Mendocinos, who have been blessed by this climate, are free of many diseases which abound in other countries".

He was quite intrigued about the Zonda, a hurricane which blows in summer and has been called "the terror of Mendoza". When this wind blows, the terrified villagers shut themselves up in their homes, close all doors and windows and light the candles as if night had fallen. The blazing gusts appear like vomit from hell, and the temperature can soar twenty degrees in no time.

The doctors were of the opinion that the population was very backward concerning general knowledge, in spite of the fact that they considered themselves naturally disposed to learn and acquire cultural notions. This was a far more benign judgement than Darwin´s, who stated: "I fully agree with Head (Francis Bond) when he says that the fate that happily awaits all Mendocinos is to eat, sleep and be lazy". Head went even further and added: "people here are extremely indolent. Whenever I walk by a house I hear snoring...until well past siesta time".

But what most surprised Head was what he saw in the Alameda, where "...crowds of women of all ages, lacking all sorts of clothing, bathed together in the stream bordering the boulevard. Shakespeare tells us that "even the most cautious maid is quite generous when exposing her charms in the moonlight", but the ladies of Mendoza, not content with that, are quite ready to show their charms to the sun, both in the morning and the afternoon..."

On the other hand, the doctors commented to Miers that San Juan was undergoing great changes, and that an English missionary had installed a Lancaster school for 300 pupils.

Doctor Gillies was bent on bringing about "positive improvement in the people", and insisted that ladies were not to be excluded from men´s social gatherings. That way, the men became gradually more willing to mingle socially with women, specially in *cafés*.

And "...women became gradually worthy of a consideration which had been denied to them in the past".

Miers commented that among the *criollos*, a woman was considered a mere domestic object that received due attention only when her favors were solicited.

Doctor Gillies managed to found a school for girls. Also a kind of literary guild and a library. Nevertheless, the enthusiastic expansion of "liberal ideas" alarmed the fanatic church representatives who took severe measures against these useful establishments and had them abolished. Doctor Gillies was allowed to stay thanks to his discreet behavior and his caution during all these proceedings. Thus the girls´ school was also saved.

Some time later, the counter-revolution brought about drastic changes, so when John Miers went again to Mendoza, in 1825, he was happy to see that Doctor Gillies was once again in charge of the literary guild and the library.

John Miers was a keen observer. During a visit to a vineyard, he remarked on the excellent quality of some of the wines –red or white- that were prepared for the consumption of *Mendocino* families, and that "if prepared with adequate care, this place could produce wines as good as those of any other place on earth, and much cheaper than those of wine- producing countries in Europe". He also commented that excessive watering of the vines produced an increase in production to the detriment of flavor. All these were his logical deductions, specially when he saw so much land under water.

He said as much to Don Juan de la Cruz Vargas, head of the Post Office to whom he presented letters of recommendation from London. He also bore letters for General San Martín, who greeted him warmly. Miers described him as a tall, well-built man. Straight-backed and broad of shoulders, tan complexion and a sharp, penetrating look. He had dark hair and large sideburns. He spoke fast and with ease. His manner was quiet and polite. He offered all the help he should need and a letter of recommendation for General O´Higgins, the highest authority in Chile. He asked him around to his house that same evening. Miers returned accompanied by Don Cruz Vargas and San Martín´s aide-de-camp, Don Ildefonso Alvarez. San Martín greeted him in a most polite fashion. They talked about grenades and other types of projectiles; he was most inquisitive about the subject and made all sorts of questions. Then he excused himself because he had to attend the social gathering that, according to the Governor´s wife, had been postponed. He then invited him to return the following morning to get the letter for O´Higgins.

The letter to O´Higgins was dictated in Miers´ presence. While the secretary took it down Miers had a close look at a splendid miniature of San Martín hanging between two portraits: one of Napoleon Bonaparte and the other of Lord Wellington, all three framed in exactly the same way.

Later, San Martín led his visitor into a small room. He opened a closet and displayed twenty very fine shotguns, rifles and hunting arms. They also spoke about the topography of the province and shared other topics of mutual interest. When they parted he once more offered his services for whatever he should need, and said they would have the pleasure of meeting again in Chile.

Miers could hardly imagine at the time that he would later achieve a deeper knowledge of this personage who would become the main actor of extraordinary political events in the future.

Miers got together with don Cruz Vargas once more, before launching on the expedition to Chile. He admired Vargas and wrote: "the more I got to know him the better I liked him. He was a man of firm character and his general knowledge was far beyond what one could have expected of the average Mendocino; he had liberal ideas about government… he was fully aware of how backward his people were from the cultural point of view, and expressed a firm desire to promote the founding of new schools. He also realized the Church was totally against such desirable measures and would do anything in its power to oppose them. He assured me that the most intelligent patriots were fully conscious of this dangerous influence and were ready to fight against the forces that tried to smother progress. He thought General San Martín was a fervent ally of education, and had already started to work in Mendoza reforming the church, getting the monks out of their convents –which he turned into military quarters- and enlisting many of the friars under his command.

He overheard that many people were against San Martín´s decision to recruit slaves. Still, he considered it was absolutely• necessary because "…although Americans are the best for cavalry, this is not the case when we consider the infantry (…). Only the colored people are really useful for this arm…"

There were many slaves in Mendoza, and when San Martín recruited the men it produced an imbalance as regards the women. In Miers´s opinion (another of the many opinions that made people dislike him): "The abundance of all that is necessary to live, the large amount of slaves and the warmth of this climate, all this has turned the fanatic and ignorant people of Mendoza into a community which is lazy, proud and selfish".

Miers also noted that *Mendocinos* always expressed a certain "…active interest in political affairs… showing a remarkable similarity to the people of Buenos Aires". General San Martín assured him that he considered this such a turbulent spirit that it was necessary to establish a real espionage system in Mendoza. In fact, he had a daily report about the thoughts and acts of the *Mendocinos*. He was aware of everything: even the most insignificant facts of each family became known to him; nobody could escape from the ever watchful eyes of his spies. The General had always been prone to secrecy and intrigue; he himself once confided that his closest friends were those who least knew his feelings; that nobody, except himself, was in touch with his spies; that nobody, except himself, was aware of this, or that… Apparently he was a kind of tyrant during his stay in Mendoza –everybody was afraid of him- and after the battle of Maipú he would have been able to rule over all the province of Cuyo, except for the fact that his ambition was targeted higher.

John Miers was very upset when he heard that don Cruz Vargas had fallen into disgrace and had been banished from Mendoza. "He had been a friend of General San Martín and his constant companion...they had spent many evenings together with a bowl of punch, to which they were both very partial". Cruz Vargas was an inveterate gambler. Miers never knew why he fell into disgrace: "I never heard the underlying motive; all I could find out was that he and General San Martín had had a very serious argument".

Next morning Miers got up in a bad mood: "Last night, when I retired to my quarters, I was again tormented by bugs. More than at other times, in fact, and my patience and tolerance weren't up to the mark. I was forced to rise, get dressed and stay up all night, alternately reading or writing, sitting on a chair or walking around".

He and his group of followers —eight men- were preparing to cross the cordillera, but they were forced to alter their plans —something which frequently happened to all those travelers organizing an expedition to Chile- because the guides didn't show up at the prearranged time. The mules had to be loaded at 11 a.m. and the guides only appeared at 5 p.m. And, as they needed at least one hour to load the mules, it turned out that when they were ready to part it was well after 6 p.m. Among those leading the march was Dr. Ward, who was brusquely overthrown by a spirited mule that took off at a gallop. Mateo Bera, the muleteer, chased the mule and managed to bring it back but, strangely enough, all Dr. Ward's luggage had disappeared: a plaid rug, a few guns, a couple of leather wine containers and a woolen bundle with clothes and other items.

Miers suspected it would be difficult to retrieve those objects. Then his own mule ran away and disappeared, together with the luggage, into some grazing lands. Again Mateo Bera went after it, brought the mule back and declared none of Miers' belongings were to be found: neither the English blankets nor his clothes, nothing. Even though Miers's found it rather surprising that both he and Dr. Ward had lost all their belongings in exactly the same way, he admitted that he was still "very naïve" and believed in Mateo Bera's words.

Among the travelers who were bound for the cordillera it was common knowledge that the muleteers and the peones were generally not to be trusted. But Miers ruefully accepted the fact that he had no choice in the matter.

Shortly before Miers's departure, don Cruz Vargas sent two of his slaves laden with presents for him to take on the journey: fruit, grapes and dried figs, biscuits, charqui, onions and tongues. Nevertheless, during all the preliminaries of his journey, Miers was doubtful whether or not to travel. After all, his friends and acquaintances were right in opposing this venture at that precise moment: his wife was already eight months pregnant, and it was really too dangerous to attempt crossing the cordillera under those circumstances.

Even Mr. Halsey, the North American Consul in Chile, who had dined with the couple before going to Buenos Aires, tried to dissuade Mrs. Miers in this matter "…he gave a most gruesome description of the mountain passes", he stressed all the possible dangers they could encounter, and made it quite clear that if she went on this journey she was risking her life

Mrs. Miers listened to him quite unperturbed and then announced that she had already taken the decision to cross over to Chile.

Miers then explained: "…a woman endowed with such uncommon courage is not easily daunted. I left the matter in her hands and she decided to carry on with the original plan".

On the way they met an officer who was traveling from Chile, who assured them the roads were in fit condition because he didn´t find snow.

They left Mendoza behind and, after marching for approximately ten leagues, Miers wrote: "…we entered the mountain range, and two leagues further we suddenly found ourselves completely surrounded by very abrupt stone walls covered in bushes and low trees with hummingbirds fluttering among the branches. We were marveled by the view. This landscape which was new to us aroused our keenest fantasies". Up to that moment the sun had been quite bearable, but once they entered a dark, narrow valley they were enveloped by a thick, damp fog that wet their clothes. As from that moment, Mrs. Miers began to feel fatigue, until she fainted on her mule. She went very pale and started feeling terrible pains. Miers was terrified that his wife could be going into labor right there; however, they did manage to walk for a short distance until they reached a shelter in Villavicencio. He put his wife on the only bed available, a rickety and not too clean cot belonging to Antonio Fonseca, the keeper. John lay down on the ground, resting his head on his saddle. Even though he was fully dressed, and covered by several blankets, the cold kept him awake all night. The room lacked a door, and the cabin itself was unprotected from the freezing wind.

Shortly after, Doctor Ward assisted Mrs. Miers in childbirth. He tried to comfort his patient, but the cold was so intense that his shivers and the chattering of his teeth prevented him from saying the soothing words he usually prepared for these occasions. In any case, Mrs. Miers´ showed great fortitude during the process and gave birth to a baby boy.

Her husband remembered that "...the little one was wrapped in swaddling clothes and put to rest in the keeper´s cot. Then he was washed and dressed by Dr. Ward".

John Miers waited for his wife to recover, hoping to return to Mendoza as soon as possible. Meanwhile, he was worried about the men he had brought with him from England -an engineer and several craftsmen-, so he finally decided to ask them to continue the journey to Chile, taking with them all the tools and instruments. These men didn´t know the country, neither did they speak Spanish. To make matters worse, they were puzzled by all these confusing episodes that had so complicated their lives since their arrival in Mendoza, which was supposed to be their haven after the exhausting trip across the dry, inhospitable pampas... What bad luck! Now, here they were, enclosed within these incredibly high mountains, deep precipices and narrow, dangerous trails... Not to mention the extreme cold that alternated with the blazing heat!

Miers´ main worry was that the freighter that was bringing the heavy machinery from England was due any moment in Valparaíso. These goods could not be disembarked in his absence. He was worried the delay would make transit through the mountains impossible and that they would be forced to wait until October or November to resume their trip. While he paced up and down pondering on all these matters he started to study the local flora, which excited his curiosity. This botanical interest helped to take his mind off his worries, at least for a while.

He also studied Fonseca´s attitude. The keeper of the shelter was always on the lookout lest any outsider should make a suspicious move. His job was to prevent animals from being stolen. Besides, he had to make sure that there always were fresh horses for hire in case travelers needed them.

The shelter consisted of three miserable ranchos: Fonseca´s room, now occupied by the Miers, a soot-covered kitchen and another room which was used by travelers to sleep in.

During the day there was quite an intense traffic of troops on mules: some bound for Chile, others for Mendoza. There was a Frenchman, a fencing master, who was going to enlist in the revolutionary navy in Chile; an *estanciero* from Calamuchita (Córdoba) who said that in the past he had given lodging to some prisoners of General Beresford´s army.

A certain Martínez, lieutenant of the 1st. Regiment of Cazadores de los Andes, was traveling with a woman. According to Miers "…he had left a wife in Buenos Aires and had joined his new companion in Chile (…) I was soon bored with his stories because he claimed to be the villain that Spain sent to Peru as sergeant of a troop on the ship "La Trinidad". He, aided by another fellow, had closed the hatchways and killed all the officers as they climbed up on deck. He seemed very proud of what he´d done and bragged about having killed thirteen officers with his own hands. On board there were 220 soldiers and 100 sailors who joined him in the mutiny; they sailed to Buenos Aires, where they were greeted with cheers…"

That afternoon, a Lieutenant Coronel Torres stopped by on his way to Chile. According to Miers, "he was a very clever *Criollo*, a very pleasant man who spoke quite good French and English…his witty conversation kept us entertained in the midst of that solitude".

In Miers´ opinion, the *gauchos* of Buenos Aires and the Chilean *guasos* were the best and strongest soldiers in the world. And he added that no other soldier would put up with the fatigue and the privations to which they had been accustomed since they were born. They were brave and easily disciplined. If they were under the orders of courageous and qualified officers no european would be able to resist them. When it came to organizing revolutionary troops, the problem was finding proficient officers.

"Torres —wrote Miers- had fought with the English army in Spain during times of extreme privations. However, he said that even our most courageous veterans seemed like pampered children when compared with the South American soldiers".

Torres was aware that the Englishmen were practically out of provisions. So when he left, he insisted on leaving them meat and bread.

That evening there was a terrible hailstorm, with thunder and lightning and Miers hoped that Torres was out of its reach. That night "…it rained through the roof in our room; water came down in buckets, it almost reached my wife who was lying with the baby on the mattress. We did everything in our power to keep the bed from getting wet. Fonseca gave us some hides he used as a mattress, and, with Doctor Ward´s help we built a sort of canopy which protected my wife and son from the rain".

The next morning was very cold and foggy. Snow covered the mountains and the area surrounding the shelter, immobilizing the men. They felt cold and downhearted. Miers said he didn´t recall ever having been so cold. At midday it started to clear up and they went to the stream to wash the clothes that the sun dried.

"My wife´s fortitude never left her; she was happy and improving rapidly; she felt so much stronger that she managed to remain sitting up for quite a few hours; her appetite was good but, to my dismay, the only food we had was some moldy bread, dried tongue, *tasajo* and tea with no milk…"

To make matters worse, the peón Miers had sent to Mendoza came back without provisions. "Don Cruz Vargas was absent, and as the stupid messenger didn´t find Doctor Colesberry at home he returned without even leaving a message, bearing the same letter I had sent him with".

Suddenly Mrs. Miers health began to deteriorate: she had fever and, unfortunately, her bed collapsed. "It was rotten. We had to carry her to Fonseca´s bed. Fonseca was worried because he´d been out hunting and returned empty-handed, which meant there was nothing to cook a meal with. It was a lovely day, the sun was shining but the air was still very cold… Things would have been more tolerable if we´d had enough food".

Miers sent the peón once again to Mendoza, to see Doctor Colesberry. His mission was to find a woman who could act as nurse. He had to get foodstuffs and other supplies as well. And he was not to return without seeing the doctor first.

"During the night —wrote Miers in his notes- her fever went up; she was restless and couldn´t sleep and, what was most alarming, her milk seemed to be gradually disappearing, in which case it would be impossible to find a substitute for the baby".

Miers was desperate. His wife´s fever, which wasn´t going down, plus the bad weather and the snow that had them immobilized threatened to impair his presence of mind. "There were people who were passing through Villavicencio on the way to Mendoza, and one would think they might have come to our aid. But…in these regions of South America nobody, be it man or woman, would go out of their way just to give a helping hand. In Europe this would never have happened. We could have stayed on and died here…".

Nobody knew the reason for Mrs. Miers´ high temperature. Miers, with bitter fatalism, jumped to the most feared conclusion: "…she seemed to have puerperal fever, a disease after childbirth from which, even in England, nine of ten women died".

At midday it started raining again. Miers tried to hide the fact that he was getting more and more depressed as time went by. But then in the afternoon their luck seemed to change: to his relief, he saw the peón returning. A married couple came with him, and they brought food and other essential supplies. The woman was a wet nurse! Doctor Colesberry had unsuccessfully tried to find a wet nurse, and it seems General San Martín had taken a personal interest in the problem. He contacted this woman and insisted she came out here to help out in this predicament. Says Miers: "If it hadn´t been for General San Martín, we wouldn´t have made it".

"But, -Miers pointed out- when I say wet nurse, let us not for an instant imagine a young, pleasant girl who is healthy, clean and eager to offer her services. Oh, no! This was an unkempt looking woman, with her head and part of her face covered with a woolen shawl and whose first impulse, on arrival, was to sit down and drink mate. The moment my wife set eyes on this woman she decided not to give her the baby for breast-feeding. But I firmly insisted she should, for her own good, and it was not without difficulty that I finally convinced her to let me put the baby in the woman´s arms".

But it wasn´t in Miers´ character to be tolerant. Analyzing the situation, it is obvious that they had received help; somehow, the baby was being fed, and, although their situation was precarious, his wife´s health didn´t get worse. Not for one second did Miers stop to consider it might have been unwise to go on this journey.

At Miers´s request, Colesberry sent a group of *peones* to carry Mrs. Miers, on a stretcher they improvised with wooden poles. Thus, they began their slow, arduous walk to Mendoza. They had difficulty in climbing down the mountain. The sun was very strong and it was hard finding their way down a rocky path. Miers and doctor Ward took turns with the peones carrying the stretcher. The Englishmen were exhausted when they finally reached Mendoza. The skin had peeled off their shoulders and their feet were full of sores.

Miers said that when they saw the city belfry at a distance, he experienced a sensation so agreeable and pleasant as he´d never felt before.

Mrs. Miers stayed in Mendoza for six more months. During that time, her husband was in Chile installing the factory. Mrs. Miers was lodged in the house belonging to "...a widow called Ricabaron, who had once been in a good financial position –explained John Miers-; they were very decent people and related to one of the leading families in Chile; her husband had been in the army and died a few years ago; being very young she was left a widow with her present family, consisting of three daughters and a son, all of them now grownup; another son had been in the army and died in the battle of Maipú... however, due to her modest social standing and because she lacked the adequate number of slaves that would make her "respectable", she was now ignored by those prominent families that had been friendly towards her when she was well off". Her daughters´ main occupation was making military belts and flags. In this they were very efficient and had earned a very good reputation: the widow was an excellent dyer; she used plants and flowers - following the indian fashion- to prepare her dyes which were bright and colorfast. Miers pointed out that the young ladies had been most kind to his wife during the six months she stayed at their house. In fact, both mother and daughters used to compete with one another in their attentions towards Mrs. Miers. Besides, they were very grateful for all the useful things she was able to teach them concerning many subjects. "None of our acquaintances visited; neither did she call on any of the prominent families in Mendoza; the motives underlying this behavior were cleared up later, although many women who afterwards apologized to her tried to justify their attitude on the grounds that she lived with the Ricabaron family that was, in a way, looked down upon since the change in their social standing". John Miers reached the conclusion that "the ignorance, pride and pretentiousness of the women of Mendoza were unbearable".

One month after having reached Mendoza on his journey from Buenos Aires, John Miers went to Chile, leaving his wife and son behind, and returned six months later to fetch them.

He parted one morning, at dawn, in the company of Doctor Ward and the muleteer. Later on they were joined by a "...sort of deserter officer who had served as a major in the revolutionary army, and his aide". They spent the first night in Villavicencio; the next day in Uspallata; the third day in Peñón Rajado, the fourth in Las Leñas and on the fifth day they got to La Cumbre, which is the highest of all the Andean range (at that point, 3.700 meters).

He observed the herdsmen used to cross the Cumbre either at dusk or at dawn; the reason was to avoid the ice-cold winds that blast with extraordinary violence across the main range between 10 a.m. and 4 p.m., making the voyage an almost impossible mission. At high altitudes it´s easy to get mountain sickness; some people try to prevent it by eating plenty of onions and avoiding alcohol; many others believe wine is the best antidote in these cases.

They passed by the corrals of the Asentistas, a slave-trading company that transported Africans to sell in Chile. The slaves, in shackles, were put in separate cells and under strict surveillance. The cells were built with loose stones, lacked doors and ceiling and were so small they could barely fit a body lying down.

Miers compared maps and references to check on the course of the expedition. When they were trudging along a certain pathway, some herdsmen told him a story that they themselves had learnt from their ancestors. Apparently, long before the Spanish conquest that route had been used by the *Incas* for their incursions in the provinces of Aconcagua. Their purpose was to collect taxes and transport stocks to the northern regions for their upkeep. These visits were celebrated with great pomp.

"General San Martín has repeatedly assured me that the story was bound to be true, because he himself had given the order to cover that road along a certain distance at a time when he had considered the idea of invading Peru by the "route of the Incas". Information revealed that the road was in good condition; water springs were to be found every now and then; this pathway was used for the transit of llamas and alpacas that carried corn to the mining centers.

On the way, Miers carried out a thorough examination of the characteristics of the soil, the passes, hills and rivers and geological formations. He also classified the flora and fauna and kept a record of climate oscillation, giving a detailed account of all specific differences. An accurate measurement of distances was all important to this man, who had already grown used to depending on his own resources because, in his opinion, "information coming from native guides was not trustworthy". In spite of the fact that he acknowledged a certain expertise in peones and muleteers when it came to solving practical problems, it was obvious that he neither liked nor trusted them. But he grudgingly admitted that there were several occasions when they were able to overcome serious drawbacks thanks to the ingeniousness of these people. For instance, once they had to cross some water courses which were too deep for them to wade through and too dangerous on account of the strong current. The muleteers were accustomed to these situations, and, using leather strips and some wood, they improvised a footbridge. Of course it was quite precarious and had to be handled with great care. The footbridge was made out of leather strips which were tied to wooden stakes on each river bank. Wooden planks were then put side by side spanning the width of the river. Once the footbridge was finished it could measure up to five meters long and one and a half meters wide. The safest way to cross it was to walk slowly down the middle. Walking on the sides was dangerous because the structure could easily tilt. This was particularly tricky when the mules crossed over with their cargo, and it was often a lasso deftly handled that saved the animals from being swallowed by the crashing waters.

When it was Miers´ turn to cross this do-it-yourself bridge, he admitted to feeling very insecure on his own two feet, so he decided to crawl on his hands and knees. And then he saw that the muleteers were on the alert because the peón following him had been on the verge of falling and was quickly saved by a timely lasso tied around his body.

Miers pointed out that it was in that precise spot that San Martín had had two forts built, each one with two cannons, apparently for defensive purposes.

The traveler had to show his papers at a control station installed by the *Mendocino* authorities. Two men were in charge of this post. According to the traveler´s notes, these men had no house or shelter where they could find protection against the strong, freezing winds and were exposed to all sorts of hardships. That was too much for Miers, who was a severe judge: "Here we have a vivid example of the indolence of these people, who, even having all the necessary elements at hand, couldn´t be bothered to spare four hours of their time to build a simple hut". He also expressed indignation when referring to the low-class people who don´t mind living in the open air, like brutes, spending all day under the blazing sun and at night, sleeping on the ground…and whose only occupation is smoking, drinking and gambling. Miers couldn´t understand how these men used a piece of leather to cover their heads as the only means of protection from blizzards or hailstorms or the heavy snowfalls which were so frequent in the cordillera.

He was full of praise for the mules, though, "…no animal walks as carefully as the mule. Although slow in its movements, it is always watchful and on the alert".

He also noted that the mule is an expert swimmer and, if it should by any chance be carried away for a stretch by strong currents, it will surely recover in no time. He admitted there were natives who were excellent riders and were never afraid when riding a mule

Crossing the cordillera was one of the most significant experiences in Miers´s life. It urged him to write a handbook with useful hints and precise instructions for any traveler who would take on such a venture in the future. He told this imaginary traveler what supplies he should take on the voyage and the proper way to pack them; how to light a fire with mule dung; the accurate distances between strategic places along the Mendoza-Santiago de Chile route. He worked out a chart with the barometer marks in inches, thermometer degrees, heights over sea level measured in feet, and average altitude. Also, a detailed description of the main passes –Deheza, Los Patos, Portillo, Planchón and Antuco- and their characteristics.

They reached Chile at mid-morning of the eighth day. The men were anxiously waiting for them in Santiago de Chile.

John Miers crossed the cordillera on four different occasions.

In 1825: after managing his firm in Chile, where he came up against no end of conflicts, he decided to return to London, and his friends urged him to write a book. Intriguing aspects of his personality were revealed in his written accounts. In his notes he often expressed opinions which offended patriotic feelings in South America. Sometimes he got carried away by irrational fits. And, what was most surprising, he made no mention of his young wife, not even her name… On that occasion he had to interrupt the writing of his *Travels* and return to Buenos Aires.

The government of Rivadavia had contracted him to build the mint; he remained in the Río de la Plata from 1826 until 1831. He had a favorable opinion of the Revolution and considered that it would gradually bring forth new energy in the criollos; it would lead them eventually towards action, thus producing a gradual expansion of the strength and the natural resources of the land.

Regarding evolution, he wrote: "…it will be quicker or slower in coming, depending on whether it is related to instruction and liberal ideas or to fanaticism and tyrannical governments; under the most favorable circumstances, its riches will come to light producing power and influence only through an increase in the level of instruction of the population. Unless an appeal to immigration is put into practice, increase of population density will necessarily be slow. In this sense, we must now wait for the results of the experiment that is being carried out both in Buenos Aires and in Entre Ríos". In Miers´ opinion, this country would gain in world-wide respect if and when it put the government in the hands of "people of good faith and liberal ideas, -an axiom which was only being considered in Buenos Aires-".

In 1831 he traveled to Brazil, where he was also contracted to build a mint; in 1833 he returned to England, this time for good. England had high regard for his scientific research, specially all that was related to earth tremor, variations in seawater level and his valuable collection of birds and insects.

But what was undoubtedly the object of his utmost care and dedication was the conservation of autochthonous plants; he made a point of illustrating the samples with very accurate and meticulous drawings. In the end, botany turned out to be his true vocation, and one of his achievements was a more efficient system for classifying valuable samples of both Argentine and Brazilian flora.

The research he carried out regarding argentine flora has been, undoubtedly, Miers´ main contribution to our country.

In 1843 he was elected a member of the Royal Society.

4.- "SUBLIME PASSAGE OF THE CORDILLERA"

Robert Proctor, the writer, arrived in Buenos Aires in 1823, in the company of a group of men and women, and his small child. They were bound southwards, with the idea of crossing the Andes and visiting Chile.

He hired the services of a government "courier", that is, guides with experience in organizing caravans or expeditions and who took on full responsibility: they hired *peones*, prepared the horses and carriages, provided the necessary supplies for the voyage, etc., etc.

Proctor was particularly intrigued about the *peones*, whom he described as "...uncultured men, but excellent riders". He closely observed their outfit, noting the soft texture of the ponchos, the incredible smoothness of their *potro* boots -which they put on while the leather was still wet and then sewed them at the point-, and the big iron spurs which were "...a terrible torment for the horses. I've seen their flanks lacerated and swollen like sponges. I have also followed carriages by the trails that blood oozing from their wounds left on the ground".

Peter Schmidtmeyer, also a writer, had traveled to the cordillera two years before. Like all Europeans who crossed the Andes, he had enormous admiration for the mules and deplored the ill treatment they got from their riders. "They're terribly cruel to animals; the reason for this is not so much the work of passion, but the lack of feeling and the tendency to give vent to their inner fire". And he finishes his observation: "A caress given to a child, or a horse, or a dog, that's something I never saw in South America.... I have seen people laugh at other peoples' afflictions, or misfortunes". He often witnessed animals being beaten to death, or left to die a slow, painful death. These things made him feel sick at heart.

The long journey across the *pampa* to Mendoza seemed to Proctor "a thousand miles of what could be the least interesting country in the world; very few things exciting enough to break up the monotony of these endless, uninhabited plains".

He was one of the few English travelers who refrained from comparing the *pampa* with an "ocean" or a "sea". He was obviously not moved –poetically speaking- by this arid landscape. On the other hand, Charles Brand, who followed the same route some time later, compared the relay station that appeared on the horizon to a "strange sail, like a ship at sea" He also wrote that they "sailed" in an ocean where "land" was always in sight.

But Proctor still had hopes. He waited with nervous anticipation for the moment of the "sublime crossing of the cordillera", which he expected would make up for the other less agreeable aspects of his journey.

He enjoyed his stay in Mendoza. His attention was drawn by the amount of irrigation channels that "fertilized" the city, its lovely gardens and the delicious muscatel grapes. He was pleasantly surprised by this modern city, which "thanks to the liberal sponsorship of general San Martin and Dr. Gillies' scientific care, has become a symbol of progress for the other cities of South America".

A Lancaster school was founded in Mendoza during Proctor's stay. And a public library was inaugurated. He observed that "…some young men were publishing a newspaper to spread liberal ideas. Profits were used to finance the school, which was annexed to a rudimentary theater where these same young people sometimes acted. These institutions had been opposed by the church and other fanatic, narrow-minded people. Nevertheless, thanks to General San Martín's patronage, the voices of these enemies of progress finally fell silent".

Proctor had letters of introduction in his power, thanks to which he was able to contact San Martín on several occasions. "San Martín frequently came to our meetings; he always amused us with interesting anecdotes. He was a remarkable story-teller, captivating his audience with his expressive face and his eloquence…He seemed as attached to Mendoza as its inhabitants were attached to him".

As a rule, all travelers were delighted with the Alameda and the vineyards, and Proctor was no exception. He described the *Mendocinas* as "bright and graceful. However, they suffer from goiter which quite disfigures their looks. I think this comes from drinking the snow water that comes down the mountain; there's hardly a woman completely free from this disease".

On the other hand, seen from a different angle, he considered this city as "one of the healthiest places in the world, with remarkably pure air".

But he eventually felt impatient to climb the cordillera, so he took care of the last details before resuming their journey: they hired thirteen mules, and acquired warm clothing, provisions and special saddles for the women (with straps to secure them on the back of the mule, and a small wooden board to rest their feet on).

They left one morning at dawn. Two hours later they were trudging through a sand desert. The heat was unbearable; when they were approaching the cordillera the ground became rough and rocky, its surface cracked due to the thaw. Water was scarce. It was only in the evening that they got to a very meager stream. All of them, men, women and the mules, pounced on the trickle of water, which did not satisfy their needs, not by a long run.

They went by "a hut called Villavicencio..." In Proctor's opinion it was "just a miserable shack that could barely be called a house", which was no other than the shelter where Mrs.Miers had given birth to her son.

The English writer was most intrigued by the food eaten by the *peones*. In fact, they only ate *charqui*, which they used to prepare "...putting it into boiling water with some red peppers, and cooking it until it turned into a sort of thick soup".

The muleteer offered them some hot *charqui*, but they turned it down. They far preferred "a pitcher of hot punch made with white *Mendocino* wine, which they drank before retiring to bed".

Proctor never ceased to show his unvarying admiration for the mules, which "were so wise when it came to choosing the safest places to tread on: every now and then they stopped to study the ground, trying to calculate the best way to avoid a crack or to reach the rock on the opposite side. Once they chose the spot they stood firmly on their hind legs while testing the ground with their fore legs. They only stepped forward when they knew they were treading on safe ground. (...) The climb is so gradual when they go up the icy surface of the mountains that the rider feels absolutely safe; now then, if he happens to look down to either side of the path, then he will suddenly grasp the real danger of the situation..."

All travelers, without exception, were thankful for the mules' self-preservation instinct. It was their own guarantee against accidents, specially when they marched at a walking pace along paths that were barely 30 cms. wide. In fact, the riders' only concern was to avoid looking down either side of the path lest a view of the heights could make them feel dizzy.

Proctor was full of admiration for the mules in spite of the fact that one had turned out to be "...a perfect demon, that resorted to no end of tricks in order to get rid of me".

He found the "little wooden crosses here and there..." rather disturbing.

They pointed to the exact spot where some unfortunate person had fallen down the cliff. He also cringed inwardly when he came across those narrow, winding paths along which the mules had to sort their way among loose stones, bordering very, very deep precipices.

Close observation of the mules´ behavior gave Proctor a certain insight as to the animals´ way of reasoning. If the mule sensed that "…the side of the load next to the mountain should bang on the rock it would inevitably throw it down the precipice, then it tried to remain on the same edge of the path and there are never two free inches between its hoof and the edge; this means that a half of the mule´s body and one of the rider´s legs are above the precipice; the terrain sometimes recedes under the animal´s step, but the mule examines the trail with great patience and caution and then deliberately places one leg in a straight line with the other". During the moments of extreme danger Proctor left his mule to its own devices, certain that it would deftly find its way through.

Whenever the group reached a relay station the women were so tired they could barely walk; during the climb they rode facing the mountain, because if their legs were on the opposite side they would feel their bodies as if suspended in space.

Any dizzy spell or a slackening of the saddle would be enough to send the lady over the precipice; therefore, if she advanced facing the mountain she couldn´t visualize the danger; what´s more, if she should fall it would be on the mountainside, which is far less dangerous.

Some paths were so narrow the travelers prayed they didn´t come across a party coming from the opposite side. Not only was it impossible for them to cross each other, but there were certain places where even turning back was out of the question.

In some stretches the riders dismounted and advanced on foot, each one with his mule leading the way. After overcoming several dangerous stretches most travelers were anxious to reach the relay station. This, according to Proctor, "with the exception of my little boy who was doing remarkably well and didn´t want to part from the peón who had been hired to carry him on the mule".

When they finally reached the station: "we prepared a light meal, because it was necessary to eat plenty of onions and drink wine as protection against the cold and the *soroche* (mountain sickness), both of which often make travelers faint".

The writer concluded that "all in all, it was an inconceivably wild spectacle".

He actually didn´t miss a single detail. It was in his nature to be very meticulous, like the time when, by request of General San Martín, he carried out a survey of a suitable route to facilitate the crossing of the troops to Chile.

In another of his anecdotes, Proctor tells how he came across the body of an Englishman who, very unwisely, had been traveling on foot and on his own. He was killed by some highwaymen and his bones still lay in a hollow of the mountain rock. Their whiteness contrasted with the black stones…there was a small wooden cross marking the spot where he had been murdered. Nevertheless, Proctor had his doubts as to the veracity of these terrible stories about the murders committed by muleteers to rob the passengers. His English friends in Chile said all this was very exaggerated.

The sight of these huge, snowcapped mountains never ceased to fascinate him. No other landscape, nothing could ever be compared to this "wild magnificence".

When Proctor reached the Cumbre he experienced a deep, weird feeling. There, at the top of these heights, he could visualize "a whole hemisphere".

Like all travelers, Proctor was intrigued by some huts that appeared every now and then along the road. These had actually been built through an initiative of Governor Ambrosio O´Higgins –in 1765- to be used as shelter by all those who happened to be caught in a storm during their journey. The huts were small –just a little over three square meters- and resembled little "ovens" because they were made of bricks and had vaulted ceilings. Built on a raised platform two meters above the ground to avoid being covered by snow, in order to get into the hut one had to climb up a small brick staircase. Unfortunately, they were all in ruinous condition: the doors, complete with frame and lintel had been wrenched off and used as firewood (the soldiers were blamed for that, apparently they didn´t feel like going out into the storm looking for wood). They were filthy and the stink was unbearable. Not only that, but icy-cold gusts of wind blasted in through holes in the walls that passed as windows, so very little was left of what was originally a shelter. Indeed, they were only used when the snow blocked the road or to seek protection during a blizzard or a rough storm. Sometimes the travelers were obliged to stay cooped up in these shacks for days as the only alternative to the possibility of freezing to death.

That was precisely the purpose for which those shelters had been built: to prevent the couriers and travelers from freezing to death in a snowstorm.

At first these shelters had boxes with coal and larders with charqui and dried food, so when the traveler got his license he was also given a key to get into the lodge and make use of the facilities it provided. But those too were thrown into the fire...

According to Proctor, all Englishmen who went by the huts took plenty of provisions along with them, not only for their own use if they chose to spend the night, but also for any other fellow traveler in need. And he added: "The natives are so lacking in foresight that they have often been found in the Andes on the verge of starvation. Although I carried an adequate cargo of supplies, the *peones* were so greedy that I couldn´t stop them from devouring the food and drinking our wine".

One morning they came across an Englishman who "...very kindly shared his provisions with us. We had dined most sparingly and had not lunched because the *peones* had eaten up all the food".

Both the keepers of the relay stations and the muleteers were also valuable sources of information. They taught the travelers all about the blizzards and snowstorms and the consequences if due precautions were not taken. They usually had a number of stories and anecdotes to illustrate their teachings, about people who got lost in a storm or a blizzard, or many others who were blockaded by snow and starved to death. A courier told them he once went through such a violent snowstorm that the cordillera had been closed down. As he was already on his way, he sought protection in one of the huts, where six of the ten people who had sought shelter had died of cold and starvation; they had eaten the mules and the dogs but it still wasn´t enough. The four that still remained alive were just skin and bones. They shivered and their teeth chattered so he couldn´t understand a word of what they were saying. Just to prove the tragedy had in fact occurred, the *peones* used to show the travelers around, pointing out the bones of the animals strewn in front of the hut.

When they were going downhill they came up against an opening next to a waterfall called Salto del Soldado. The reason for its name (Soldier´s Jump) was that when the liberator army was advancing towards Chile, a soldier deserted and was pursued by his party. When he saw he was being closed in by them, he decided to risk his life and jumped across to the other side of the rapids. He managed to get away...His pursuers didn´t dare risk their necks in the same way, they just looked on while the man who was doomed to die escaped to freedom.

In the last part of their journey, Proctor and his committee reached a stream of deep and abundant waters. The only possible way of crossing to the other side was over a rickety bridge made of wooden poles. Definitely dangerous. They all dismounted and, in a respectful imitation of the mules, learnt how to test the ground before stepping very, very slowly....

Once in Chile Proctor was able to meet Bernardo O´Higgins and speak his own language. The Chilean military man belonged to a family of Irish descent and had been educated in his ancestors´ mother country. Proctor was most impressed by his manner, he found him both "pleasant and entertaining", qualities which he thought were not easily found in times of intrigue and revolution.

The Englishman then continued on his voyage to Peru, to carry out the task for which he´d been commissioned: to negotiate a loan with the Government of that country.

5.- THE MEDITATIONS OF CALDCLEUGH

Alexander Caldcleugh was another exponent of the Personal Narrative. Originally, he had been commissioned –by official parties or private capitals, who knows...- to make a survey of the area as a commercial market and evaluate possible benefits for future investors.

Apparently, he deviated from his original mission and branched off into personal meditations and a train of thought that had very little to do with his task. He wrote a very long report suggesting –among other things- the creation of a commercial shipping line, manufacturing ponchos in order to compete with the local craftsmanship, to promote the consumption of brandy among the Indians –the Criollos had already accepted it-, etc., etc.

His long, generous reports reflect the fact that he was a curious man, he took a personal interest in everything he saw and wasn´t particularly worried whether those who read his comments shared his own enthusiasm regarding the people, their ways and habits, and the local scene.

He expressed himself in a direct and forthright manner, like in his "Travels in South America", when he accused the Paraguayan dictator Doctor Francia of holding the French scientist Bonpland captive. However, he admitted he was at a loss when he tried to describe the cordillera. He was spellbound by the "splendid and sublime" view and lacked the words that could express his innermost feelings.

But it was General San Martín´s personality and life experience that motivated his main considerations:

"All those who are aware of the degree of envy and violent hostility so common in this part of the world must logically infer that San Martín is indeed a remarkable man, because with his presence he either managed to appease those passions, or else he made good use of them for the aims he pursued.

His crossing of the Andes is usually compared to Napoleon´s feat when crossing Mt. Saint Bernard. But, considering the advantages Napoleon could count in his favor –e.g. a disciplined army and an abundance of supplies and reinforcements-, it is obvious that San Martín´s achievement is even more admirable".

Caldcleugh expressed these thoughts the day before crossing to Chile, when news had got around that the Indians were approaching. As to these, he wrote: "...After the capture in San Luis they became so arrogant that they approached Mendoza and threatened with an onslaught...under these circumstances, it was wise to retreat through the cordillera while the condition of the road made it possible".

Following his friend don Miguel Valenzuela´s advice, he went in through the southern pass el Portillo. The guide had suggested going along paths that had shelters and other facilities, but Caldcleugh insisted on Portillo because it was the most direct access (other routes were Los Patos, Uspallata and El Planchón).. He left with the guide, three mules for riding, two for carrying the luggage, five spare mules in case of an accident, and plenty of supplies.

The third day, after collecting some geological samples, they started to climb the mountain. The air felt brisk at first, then downright cold. The guide gave Caldcleugh some pebbles. The Englishman thanked him and put the pebbles in his pocket, with the intention of throwing them away when nobody could see him. But the guide said they were not to keep, they were to put inside one´s mouth as a precaution in case they were caught in a hurricane wind. Later, they arrived at the Customs in Chacalo, where he had to show his passport. The guard´s wife had a bad case of goiter. She was very busy making cheese, with her husband´s help.

That night they were unable to sleep because it started to pour and, although they all huddled in a corner, they got drenched. They also suffered a massive attack of flees and lice. To make matters worse, when they were programming a survey of the terrain for the following morning, Caldcleugh suddenly realized that the scientific instruments they carried were insufficient.

Next morning it was bitterly cold. Men shivered and, when they spoke their teeth chattered in such a way that they could hardly make themselves understood. In the meantime, Caldcleugh made a careful study of the geological characteristics of the soil and wrote everything down: "No matter where I looked, I always saw a new and most interesting view. Along the way, I collected samples and made all the geological observations I saw fit...". The guide was not so happy with what he perhaps considered to be a loss of valuable time. He was worried lest they had to suffer yet another storm or snowfall in Portillo.

Bordering a narrow, winding path "...one could see the carcasses of mules that had fallen maybe forty, or even a hundred years back, in an excellent state of preservation as if they had died only recently".

When they were riding up the mountain he dismounted to pick up samples of "an igneous substance of yellow magnesium". But he felt so weak that he soon had to get back on the mule.

The wind slapped their faces. They would have hurried just to get rid of this torture, but the path had disappeared. This set them back a few hours, until they finally found a cave and were able to take cover. The situation was quite desperate: the storm was still raging, the river they were bordering was frozen and the hungry mules had nowhere to graze. After six days they started to run short of food. There was no way of cooking the little beef that was left because of the lack of wood .

During one of the climbs the snowstorm became even more violent. The guide dismounted to explore the ground and the snow came up to his waist. One of the mules fell down a slope with all its load. Fortunately, the snow cushioned the fall and they recovered it alive. But that took them another hour and by that time the storm had got worse, with thunder and lightning and the works.

When they reached the shelter they were utterly exhausted, and afraid of frostbite.

Caldcleugh wrote: "…when I was on the mule the snow came up to my waist. The guide was very worried, he said he didn´t remember a storm as fierce as the one we were suffering".

The next day the weather improved considerably, the sun came out and the snow began to melt. They searched for roots and built a comforting fire. They put their clothes to dry.

Going downhill the Englishman took his time and continued with his geological research, much to the annoyance of the guide, whose only desire was to get to Santiago.

On the way they met some muleteers who were going in the opposite direction, and the guide described the storm they had been through. Judging from the expression on their faces, Caldleugh realized that the danger of the situation had far exceeded the discomfort which he had had to put up with.

6.- A PICTURESQUE CHARACTER

Samuel Haigh felt a shiver down his spine. There he was, walking through a very dark, narrow pass with huge rock walls on either side, when he suddenly looked down and saw human bones strewn on the ground. He looked questioningly at the guide, who explained that a fierce battle had taken place between General San Martín´s forces and the Spanish guard that was stationed there to protect the pass. Those bones belonged to the *Godos* who had died in battle and had been left there "to feed the hawks".

That evening they got to a valley where they decided to spend the night. They were placidly sitting round the fire and Haigh again brought up the subject that had made such an impression on him. He wanted to know more about the strife which, judging by the amount of bones, must have been very brutal.

He was disappointed when it became obvious that he wasn´t getting any more information from the muleteers. Was it ignorance on their part, or just another evidence of that indifference which got on his nerves?

He wasn´t on very friendly terms with them. Specially one of them "on purpose or through sheer stupidity, took great pains in molesting me and always stood just in front of me when I was sitting by the fire in our bivouacs. I disliked this habit of his and told him so repeatedly, but he always pretended not to understand. Until one day I lost my patience and I shot him with an empty bullet on his backside ...his colleagues roared with laughter". That was the second incident he had put up with up to that moment. The day before one of the guides wanted to take the mule away from him, but Haigh refused. Suddenly the Englishman was caught unawares by the muleteer who gave him a push. Haigh landed face down on the snow while the muleteer laughed and jeered at him. Haigh said nothing, swallowed his anger and secretly swore to take revenge. Some time later, the guide was standing on a hillock, gazing absentmindedly ahead, when the Englishman approached stealthily from behind, kicked him on his backside and struck a blow on his shoulder with a stick. The muleteer toppled over and reeled several meters down the snow-covered slope. "The sight of him rolling in the snow aroused hoots of laughter from his henchmen, who were getting tired of the hateful tyranny he imposed on them. At the sight of their "leader" in such a ridiculous position, they bared their teeth and laughed like hyenas".

They endured rough storms and extremely low temperatures. Fortunately, Haigh wore special snow-shoes "…made of sheepskin, tightly tied to the foot and ankle, the part of the sole protected by a thick, pliable sole that adjusts to the instep with leather straps". The muleteers provided him with *pellones* and sheepskins to put on the saddle. "We resembled a group of laps climbing to the top of the mountain".

At times the problem was the sun reflecting on the snow: "the glare almost blinded us; moreover, the cold had made our lips turn purple and swell to double their normal size, to the point that when we attempted to talk they split open and blood oozed out. These are the inevitable side-effects of traveling across the cordillera in winter; I even know of people who have remained half blind for over a week after days such as these".

In spite of the hardships he had to put up with, Haigh was usually in an optimistic frame of mind. It was rough going, and yet he always let himself fall under the spell of this magnificent landscape. Those immense rock walls that could be at times so imposing were also awe-inspiring in their magnificence.

Once, the snowfall was so intense they were forced to dismount and continue on foot. The snow covered their knees, and they seemed to have no proper alternatives: on one hand, they prayed the sun would come out. On the other hand, if it did come out they would be blinded by its reflection on the snow.

The raging wind -"its gusts seemed to penetrate our bodies"- forced them to cover their faces with shawls while they advanced, very slowly and with great effort "…along very narrow paths near the cutting edges. We again encountered many crosses like those we saw all along the way, marking the spot where some poor wretches met their death with no other funereal hymn than the shrill cry of the condors on their skeletons…"

When they were in the outskirts of Chacabuco, Haigh commented to a fellow countryman who had joined the group, that they were about to go across a place of great historical value, where the patriots under General San Martín´s command won a great victory.

Haigh finally reached Santiago (in those days, natives and muleteers referred to Santiago as Chile).

He was invited to a party that San Martín was giving in the Cabildo, in honor of Commodore Bowles, who was in command of the British fleet in the Pacific; its frigate, the "Amphion" was anchored in Valparaíso-.

7.- CRAWFORD AND HIS ENGINEERS

The firm Waring Brothers commissioned a group of civil engineers to explore and mark out the route of the Trasandino Railway. This railroad, which would join Buenos Aires with Santiago de Chile, was meant to be built during Sarmiento´s presidency. To that end they traveled to the Rio de la Plata. Robert Crawford, chief of Engineers, narrated in his book "Across the Pampas and the Andes" the sequence of events of the 1871 expedition, whose members were very excited with the idea of entering into the heart of the Andes.

Although they were all experienced professionals who had come out here to carry out a job, the idea of fancy adventures excited their imagination. Of course they were aware that they would have to travel through a very vast territory which was no more than Indian hunting grounds. But that was nothing –or so they thought- compared to the marvels that awaited them! They knew of the possible dangers in store for them, but these were underestimated, and no risk was worth considering because, after all, they would climb the colossal Andes, and explore the valleys in this famous mountain range. "Instead of using the customary paths we preferred to go through places unexplored by man; we could hardly envision the marvels that awaited us in these remote places!".

As engineers, they also felt stimulated by the fantastic projects they visualized in this wild geography and its contrasts of heights and slopes, curves and precipices.

Their problems started when the party left Mendoza; after the first two kilometers, "…the muleteers refused to continue, they unloaded the mules and calmly started setting up camp for the night; they obviously had no intention of leaving those nice places where they had lived those last days until they had run out of money and credit". And then Crawford wrote: "the discovery that one of my favorite horses had been sold in Mendoza made me feel very angry. And another horse which belonged to me personally had been given as a gift to the commissioner…".

Crawford was annoyed because although "the expedition was supposedly under my orders and control, when something was done in spite of my disapproval, government officials informed me they had acted following orders that came from higher up".

However, all these drawbacks seemed to disappear when "…our tired eyes beheld a view so grand and magnificent that fatigue was replaced by awe and wonderment. There they were, the Andes!… every instant the scene changed, and each transformation brought with it a beauty that had hitherto not been captured… It was impossible not to feel deeply moved by this view, or to find words to describe it".

They saw some condors on the way: "I shot down four with my rifle. These "big vultures" of the Andes…fly in circles examining every bit of ground, in the hope of finding some morsel to feast on. If something draws their attention they spread out their wings and hastily fly down to a lower level so as to get a closer look at the object. One morning, one of my mates put the condors´ curiosity to good use and wounded four of them in the wing. He resorted to the trick of lying still on the ground face upwards, until a condor that had been hovering over him would descend to see if it was a dead body it could feed on; when he got to shooting distance, the bird paid for such recklessness with its life".

Afterwards they bathed in a stream of clear waters but had to get out immediately because there were leeches. Apparently, one of the leeches "clung to the physician´s foot. I suppose it felt some sort of kinship with a professional colleague ".

That same night, at the postmaster´s request, the physician had to attend a man who had been knifed during a brawl. Crawford observed that "one of the worst calamities in this country is the terrible and frequent use of the knife which every *gaucho* carries in his belt".

A sheep breeder of his acquaintance told him about two *peones* who fought in his own house over an entirely unimportant matter. One of them stabbed the other right in his heart. Then he grabbed him by the hair and "dragged the dying man out into the courtyard because he said it was a shame to have bloodstains on the floor inside the house".

All these stories made an impact on Crawford, who adopted a defensive attitude. Some days back he had scolded a muleteer and asked to have him fired. However, due to the shortage of herdsmen he was forced to put up with him and postponed any disciplinary actions. But Crawford felt apprehensive about this man. He didn´t sleep well at night. Any slight noise woke him up and "…every time the noise of footsteps by my bed woke me up I invariably saw this same man who, when questioned, always answered he was looking for someone".

But other details also helped to keep Crawford awake: "some fat, cold drops of water soaked our bed clothes and slapped our faces in such a persistent way that it was impossible to sleep". The storm raged all night long and all the following morning. When they were about to leave they suddenly realized that fourteen mules and one member of the group –a Scotsman- were missing. It started to pour again and by that time they had no dry rugs or garments.

They climbed up a very steep slope and when they had set up camp and were getting ready to sleep they heard some mules braying and the noise of running feet; it was a puma that had been lured by the smell of *asado* and stealthily approached the group. Some mules got frightened and escaped and others they were able to hold back. But twenty managed to escape.

The expedition went on its way, except for a group of *peones* that went to find the mules. That night it rained heavily again and Crawford by that time was fed up with having to sleep with wet clothes and rugs.

The following day, the presence of guanacos called their attention: "…we took a few shots at them and one of the men killed one". Later they discovered that guanaco meat was not tasty (with the exception of *chulengo* meat), but the soup was delicious. They knew that guanaco hides were most appreciated by the Indians, who used them to make clothes. They decided to imitate them, and left the hides to dry. Eventually they came in useful to mend the clothes of all the members of the expedition, which were all in rags and tatters.

This newly-found activity helped to distract all those who enjoyed game hunting during their moments of leisure. "The practice of this sport was very gratifying. With my rifle, I was lucky to hunt down seven guanacos, and other companions of mine were equally successful…I think we killed over forty guanacos that day".

Crawford made it quite clear that they did not hunt down the guanacos when they were trapped and helpless between high rock walls. (Which was, incidentally, the situation that hunters usually took advantage of to carry out a mass killing of defenseless animals)

Quite the opposite, Crawford explains: "…we patiently waited for the right moment to get near our prey. Guanacos, just like deer, are hard to approach because of their wild ways, always wary and on the alert. They're not easily perceived at a distance because their color is like the ground they tread on. They have, though, a characteristic which gives the hunter an advantage over them.

They always seem to have a sentry posted (guanaco leader) that at the slightest hint of danger neighs as a sign of warning…". In Crawford's opinion, that sound of alarm was a kind of indiscretion on the animal's part because "it calls the hunter's attention towards the herd and gives him the opportunity to calculate the best way of approaching his prey".

Guanacos usually graze in high places, that way they can perceive any imminent danger; they try to pass unnoticed, which is not so difficult as their color is easily taken for vegetation, or a part of the ground. Their leader keeps watch at a distance while the rest of the group remain waiting for the sign. If it happens to see a trespasser, the guanaco leader has him under observation. If it becomes clear that there's no way out, then it will emit the sound of warning. That final neigh causes the herd to escape. The sentry assumes full responsibility for the herd. It conquered its leading position through fierce fighting against the other males. We could say the leader rightfully won his position of power by proving it is the bravest and strongest of the herd. It can only be defeated by the hunter. Meanwhile, the females protect their little *chulengos* keeping them close to the side of the body that the hunter cannot see.

While Crawford and his party were camping high up in the mountain they were found by an army patrol of twenty soldiers that had been sent from Fort San Rafael to escort them. And, to everybody's amazement, with them was the Scotsman that had been missing for eight days and that all had given up for lost. He told them what had happened: apparently his mule started to buck, threw him off and galloped away carrying his rifle. He was left on foot, far from the rest of the group and without food; thinking it was impossible to catch up with them he decided to walk to the Fort.

They climbed down to the valley of the Río Grande. There, the soldiers refused to continue for fear of being attacked by Indians; if that were to happen, they would certainly be killed. But their commanding officer expressed his indignation and reminded the soldiers that they "were hired and paid to fight". To which a soldier candidly replied:

"But we haven't been paid!" (Everybody laughed)
"Being paid or not paid is not the point –replied the officer- You must obey orders".

Then they reached Río Tordillo, a very difficult, risky pass because it was encased between high cliffs and there was no pathway. In some stretches they had to crawl up steep slopes digging crevices for the mules to use as footholds.

Again Crawford marveled at the natural sagacity of the mules: "its intelligence is really remarkable; first it probed the ground with an extended leg to make sure it was safe, then it dug its hoof firmly before transferring the full weight of its load, and it repeated all this procedure, step by step, until the danger was over".

Suddenly the road was blocked by a huge stone and there was no way to avoid it. "One of our companions decided to try something out while we all looked on with expectancy". He made the mule approach the base of the rock, which had hardly any room to move around it. The mule took a look at the precipice, seemed to ponder and then took a decision. It pressed its side against the rock wall and then, inch by inch it went around the jutting ledge until it reached firm ground. Crawford's mule tried to do the same but a stirrup got caught in one of the jutting edges and the mule started to push and pull until it lost its balance and rolled over the slope. Crawford was certain the mule would roll all the way down to the precipice, but when he looked down: "…there was the mule, agile as a goat, heaving its weight after a six meter drop and deftly climbing up to where I was standing. If there was ever a repentant mule this was it. The shame for having caused such a mess was clearly expressed in its eyes…in the future, it was a reformed mule".

The next river they came across had water that was cold as ice because it was, in fact, melted snow. The high-mountain air was bitterly cold too. They took off their clothes and put them to dry on some stones. Meanwhile, they ran to and fro trying to keep warm and warding off a chill. But the air was so cold that they ended up putting on their still damp clothes because "…after all, it was better than nothing".

In that zone they carried out a new land survey for the building of the railroad, and pointed out that major works of engineering had to be done in Río Grande. For the first time they experienced earth tremors and they agreed that "…we can only talk about it once the moment of danger is over".

While they were carrying out the tasks they had planned in Rio Grande they came across some cattle that had cut loose from the herds that were sent to these pastures for grazing. The soldiers concluded they must have been stolen by Indians or cattle thieves, but that didn't stop them from hunting the animals down and eating them in tasty *asados*. The most expert riders put on an amusing show taming some wild mules, and they were cheered by the group of engineers.

On the other hand, Crawford also won the natives' admiration when he flung his portable rubber dinghy into the waters of the Rio Grande and sailed across to the opposite bank, while studying some rocky headland he found on the way.

That night they were assailed by a raging storm that had been gradually working up. They were unable to sleep and remained fully clothed, expecting the worst to happen.

They met with another expedition at a prearranged point. The other party had come all the way from the Pacific coast carrying out different surveys. Both groups joined forces, although maintaining their respective independence in their professional tasks. However, in certain things they worked together as a team, e.g. exchanging information, correcting and reexamining various layouts. All this under a strong, relentless wind.

Finally (at one point it was difficult to tell whether the engineers were amused or afraid), there was imminent danger of an Indian onslaught. The technicians and their escort were forced to seek protection in the Fuerte Media Luna. Then it turned out that the aborigines had disappeared through some secret passes. Could it mean that they didn´t want to add new casualties?

Nevertheless, the war of nerves had its effect on the engineers´ spirits. They were worn out, almost freezing to death, and downcast. It was in that state of mind that they resumed their journey to Curicó, Chile, the next morning.

After five months of camping out in the pampa and the cordillera, of sleeping out-of-doors and having to put up with all kinds of hardships and privations, they finally lodged at a hotel owned by a German. During the thirty six hours they spent there, they couldn´t have enough of the small luxuries it afforded, such as frequent and lengthy hot baths, much to the hotel owner´s dismay...

After their pleasant rest in Curicó they set out for Santiago.

8.- SAN MARTIN IN THE HEART OF THE ANDES

"Tonight I was introduced to General San Martín. I was most impressed by the personality of this Hannibal of the Andes –wrote Haigh-. He is tall and well built; on the whole, he gives the impression of someone who is solid and dependable. He has expressive looks and a soldierly bearing. Light tan complexion, dark hair and big sideburns with no moustaches. His big, black eyes have a fiery look and a vivacity that could under no circumstances pass unnoticed. He has the manners of a gentleman. When I saw him, he was in the middle of an animated conversation with several people surrounding him; he gave me a warm welcome, because he is very fond of the English nation".

Several of Haigh´s fellow countrymen were enlisted in the revolutionary army. With them he spoke of military events. He explained: "San Martín gave careful consideration to his plans and was, on the whole, very cautious, because the royalists had not the slightest clue as to where they had to wait for the enemy forces; in fact, they had sent part of their troops down South because they feared that the patriots would advance through Planchón or the territory of Pehuenche indians to join O´Higgins´s numerous troops in the province of Concepción. In other words, San Martín´s strategy was a masterpiece of skill and discretion, by which he was able to mislead the Spanish governor, who scattered his troops in remote, isolated sites in Chile".

In those days, English travelers –merchants, businessmen, technicians, financiers, whatever- were very up-to-date as to the political and military alternatives in the Provincias Unidas. They had to be, because being fully informed was the only way of looking after their interests. Some of them wrote their impressions in books. Their observations were at times acute and unprejudiced although seldom indulgent; other times they proved to be biased, or scornful, and even incorrect. But they were always interesting and provided useful information which could rightfully be considered as part of our historical heritage.

For instance, let´s take the case of John Miers. He was a keen observer and very crude when expressing his opinions. That is why he was criticized by so many people, and why he aroused such heated indignation in many of his readers. However, it does seem quite significant that San Martín, no less, felt real affection for this man and was most concerned about the welfare of Mrs. Miers and her baby, to the extent of sending them a wet nurse when they were stranded in the middle of the cordillera. Besides, he often appealed to the Englishman´s professional know-how in matters concerning weaponry.

English travelers had a special liking for San Martín who, in turn, was most partial to England and its people. They admired him for being a talented army man who was on the same level as any of his famous European colleagues.

Miers was impressed with the negotiation held between San Martín and the Indian Chief Maripán. Actually, San Martín had discussed it lengthily with Miers.

According to Miers, San Martín´s purpose was "...to convince Maripán that he intended to invade Chile through the southern pass Planchón, and that, therefore, he must help him with all the Indian forces he could muster. The Cacique agreed to provide support, in exchange for which San Martín had to give him one thousand mares and a certain amount of liquor, knives, beads, etc. Furthermore, the General gave him one thousand five hundred mares, plus double the stipulated amount of gifts and a beautiful scimitar set in silver. It was agreed that Maripán would organize a private interview with the Spanish general Marcó del Pont, in Chile. The idea was to deceive him as to San Martín´s plans, so he had to feed him false information, namely, that San Martín intended to cross by the passes of Los Patos and Uspallata and enter the country via the valley of Aconcagua; to make the deceit even more convincing, the patriot General promised to send guerrilla fighters to keep up a permanent threat.

The Indian Chief swore to keep all these terms in absolute secrecy; but San Martín, who was fully aware of the Indians´ treacherous nature, was convinced that the Cacique would meet Marcó del Pont and would readily accept another bribe, thus turning against him".

"In the meantime, San Martín kept sending express messengers through the Pass of Uspallata bearing false dispatches in code, with elaborate explanations of how he intended to cross the cordillera by Planchón. The Spanish general Marcó del Pont was therefore convinced that the Indian´s version was correct and expected San Martín to cross into Chile through Planchón.

Consequently, Marcó installed his main forces in Rancagua and when the expedition left Mendoza there was not a single officer or civilian who had the slightest inkling as to the pass they had to cross. That is, until they actually set forth.

The patriot troops reached Aconcagua so speedily that they launched a surprise attack on the Spaniards and routed them over the impregnable escarpment of Chacabuco, which also acted as a barrier against any forces which might be coming from the side of the capital city; and the "Army of the Andes" –name given to the revolutionary forces- reached the Chacabuco plains before the Spanish troops would have been able to move from Rancagua. The outcome of this glorious day is known to all..."

Foreigners had an overt admiration for the strategy, tactics and actions of espionage and counter-espionage displayed by San Martín. Their love of excitement and intrigue was aroused by all the tricks used with the indians. Which were also justified, according to Manuel A. Pueyrredón (military journalist and warrior who fought in the battle of Maipú) because the *Araucanos* "...declared themselves supporters of the royalist cause, fighting side by side with the Spaniards whom they referred to as "royalist companions", while they called us *pachoco tregua*, which means dog... Whenever they took some of our men prisoner they always slaughtered them (...) During an onslaught they took fourteen Negroes from us; they burnt them because Christians –they said- used them to make gunpowder".

Travelers felt that crossing the cordillera was one of the most significant experiences in their own lives. They knew what it was about... Therefore, it stands to reason that they were full of admiration for San Martín and his people in that enormous feat which meant crossing a whole army together with weaponry and equipment through that maze of rocks along impossible paths, with bottomless precipices, and an intolerable weather.

San Martín himself sent a communiqué to the government of Buenos Aires, in February of 1817, describing the essentials of his venture: "A hundred leagues of steep heights, defiles, deep and narrow passes, cut by four cordilleras. Such is the way to Los Patos... conquering it has been a real triumph".

The above mentioned four cordilleras found on the way to Los Patos were Sierra del Paramillo, Cordillera del Tigre, Cordillera de Espinacito, and Cordillera Andina –the border between Argentina and Chile-. The biggest obstacle was the river Los Patos.

That was the route followed by 10.600 mules, 1.600 horses and 700 head of cattle; all the animals were very well looked after, and yet only 4.300 mules and 511 horses managed to reach Chile. Most of them died on the way. Rugs were used to keep the mules and horses warm instead of straw. Otherwise, the animals might eat it.

Climate fluctuations were another major problem. Many of the Africans that had joined the Infantry died on account of the extreme cold to which they were not accustomed. During the day the troops traveled under the sun, putting up with temperatures of even 30° C. And at night it was freezing cold, about 10° C below zero, or more. Another big drawback was the height which, at an average of 3.000 meters, caused mountain sickness, migraine, dizziness, agitation, sensation of asphyxia and various bronchial disorders. They tried to counteract these consequences eating plenty of onions and garlic but it turned out to be a futile effort.

In the opinion of certain analysts who specialize in military matters, one of San Martín´s cleverest tricks was when he sent a communiqué to Congress stating that he had temporarily delegated the political management of Mendoza to its Cabildo, because he was going to be absent for some time. The reason he gave was that he had to travel more than one hundred leagues southward, to study the entry points of the Andes and assess which needed fortifying against a potential royalist attack.

His message had a double purpose: on one hand, disguising his offensive strategy helped to mislead Marcó del Pont´s spies; on the other hand, he pretended to be a submissive bureaucrat who informed Congress of any small, simple procedure, thus conveying the idea that he was not the kind of person who took important decisions on his own initiative.

The Spanish Command must have felt very relieved when its spies transmitted the message. The contents of the message were very clear: the patriots had no intention of launching an attack, which meant that the royalists could avoid the trouble of strengthening defensive forces in the cordillera with all it entailed as regards organization, time and expense.

The smoke screen devised by San Martín served its purpose: the Spanish Command saw no need to take active measures, thus leaving the initiative in the hands of the patriot leader who was, apparently, a docile character inclined to submissive attitudes. That was the impression San Martín wanted them to have. When he sent the message advising Congress that he was delegating the political power in order to go and "make a survey of the points of the cordillera that might prove tempting to the enemy forces occupying Chile" he concealed his real purpose, which was to obtain a first-hand impression of the andean scene in all that could interest him particularly.

The military analyst Astudillo Menéndez said that the patriot leader "…kept the main purpose of his plan completely secret, thanks to which the enemy lost its bearings and, unknowingly, lent itself to the war game in San Martín´s own terms. The royalists had to follow the rhythm of the trench warfare he imposed on them, obliging them to scatter their troops, submitting them to extenuating, useless marches and gradually undermining their morale in a permanent state of alert…".

San Martín´s record in the Napoleonic Wars, as in the battles fought in America, -added this military analyst- revealed that the main concepts underlying his operative procedures were "maneuver and initiative".

The two forts mentioned by Miers —with two cannons each- built apparently for defensive purposes, were just another of his misleading tactics, meant to give the impression that he was establishing a retaining line.

Other military analysts besides Astudillo claimed it was "a sorry gesture of naïveté", or "a legend" or "sheer fantasy" on the part of those who presumed San Martín would have entrusted records of topographic irregularities of the Los Patos and Uspallata Passes to the memory of one of his subordinates (José Alvarez Condarco).

When Alvarez Condarco —San Martín´s aide-de-camp- took a copy of the Independence Act signed in Tucumán in 1816 to show it to Marcó del Pont, it was just a pretext. His real purpose was to survey and memorize the characteristics of the terrain, but he couldn´t take notes lest he was taken for a spy. His behavior was in keeping with the mission officially commissioned to him, so he would hardly be able to remember in detail such a vast and complex information. He would have a general idea, but by no means the inch-by-inch survey that San Martín needed. All analysts coincided in that someone as brilliant as San Martín in warfare tactics and strategy "would never have made that mistake". Treatise writers sustain that without a thorough knowledge of the andean topography success would have been impossible. In other words, all the information and reports he had been able to assemble were then verified in a personal exploration which he himself carried out. Which is exactly what he had done in San Lorenzo, when, at night, he used to go over all the plains where the battle was to take place until he was absolutely familiar with the layout.

The map that San Martín displayed on his work table obviously did no justice to the magnificence of the cordillera. Quite the contrary, reducing the landscape to simple scales helped to enhance the importance of his tactics and strategy. He had to adjust his operative plan to the scenario, and that excluded all vague references or makeshift arrangements. '

The idea of crossing the cordillera into Chile and advancing from there into Peru might not have been an exclusive initiative of San Martín. But carrying it out was definitely his own merit.

Previous attempts had used the route of Alto Peru and ended in failure. There was no way of implementing a successful strategy, and the results of these incursions were numerous casualties and heavy material losses, not to mention the undermining of revolutionary morale. So, unbelievable as it may seem, the rugged, maze-like cordillera was a far more suitable scenario to carry out a military project based on sound strategy and audacious war tactics.

An endless row of soldiers climbed the cordillera with its defiles, up steep slopes, through narrow passes, always up, higher and higher until they surpassed the five thousand meters, suffering from lack of oxygen and mountain sickness, numb with cold or hot and exhausted, and always troubled by the raging, ever-present wind.

San Martín sent a small squadron southwards, just to distract the enemy's attention, and the main army corps were sent to Los Patos and Uspallata, where they were not expected.

Buenos Aires sent very little help to the revolutionary army. Therefore, the arms supply was something to be dealt with in Mendoza. They had few and rudimentary tools and the forges were very elementary. Still, the priest Fray Luis Beltrán managed to smelt the artillery items and manufactured bayonets, sabers and ammunition. And also horseshoes which were to be used for the first time in the armies of the Provincias Unidas.

On the 18th and 19th of January 1817, the leading troops initiated the crossing of the cordillera. The idea was to advance through Los Patos and Uspallata and take the royalist army by surprise. Lesser forces and patrols -whose mission was to provoke harassment and distraction among the enemies-, had to use other passes, set base in small villages and get support from the local people.

Victories in Chacabuco and Maipú were the crowning glory of San Martín's project.

9.- THE PIONEERS AND THEIR CHALLENGE

"I only stepped back a few paces –Madsen admitted-. But I took a firm stand to fight with my back to the wall (the wall was the Fitz Roy)"

In 1873 Punta Arenas was inhabited by around one hundred and fifty people whose firm determination was to rebuild this Magellian town devastated some twenty years back by Captain Cambiazo and his mutineers: his garrison and the prisoners of the military prison. They had occupied the village, taking its inhabitants prisoner. For days and nights on end the rioters lit enormous bonfires where their captives were burnt to death; they pillaged and murdered and set in motion a system of terror and lunacy. They shot Governor Muñoz Gamero and the remaining villagers were forced to leave; some of them didn´t dare look back; those who did saw what was left of their houses in flames...

The colony was burnt down. Nothing was left of what had been "the pearl of the Magellan Straits". That tragic mutiny left terrible scars which took many years to heal... As Musters once said, when visiting Punta Arenas: "...seen from a social angle, Punta Arenas must have been inconceivably sad".

In 1867, Oscar Viel was named Governor; he did his best to bring new life back to the colony, tried to attract new inhabitants; these were mostly sailors who abandoned their ships to search for gold, or to carry out commercial dealings, or maybe just to pursue a life of adventure.

As chance would have it, three men turned up in Punta Arenas simultaneously –presumably for different reasons- and became the only true capitalists of the extreme south of the Andes. They were a Portuguese sailor called José Nogueira, an immigrant from Asturias named José Menéndez, and Mauricio Braun, a Lithuanian.

They installed lumber mills, agricultural establishments, meat-packing factories, railroads, shipyards, power stations, telephones, means of transport; they had their own docks, coastal shipping fleets, stores, banks, insurance... And when possibilities of expansion in Chile reached the limit, they extended their business operations to Patagonia. They eventually installed their head office in Buenos Aires. And, in the meantime, they bought as much land as they could lay their hands on down in Patagonia. Whether they leased the land or bought it in their name or through front men, the fact is that they ended up owning millions of hectares.

José Nogueira, the Portuguese sailor, started out as a sea-lion hunter when he was only twenty. Although he was an uncouth young man with no education, he must have had plenty of inborn talent because it was Luis Piedra Buena –no less- who taught him the tricks of the trade and who, finally, made him his partner. But Nogueira wanted to become independent. To that purpose he bought a schooner and worked very hard till he had earned his initial capital. With that money he set up a general store. He traded hides and furs which he acquired from the same clients who bought tools, equipment and supplies from him.

When gold was discovered in the Chilean Tierra del Fuego, he provided supplies to the miners. Those who were unable to settle their accounts were forced to transfer the title deeds to his name. He consequently decided to organize a mining concern to exploit the gold resources in the region, and, as it couldn't be otherwise, he was the main shareholder of the company.

He also founded a company for the rescue of ships in danger of being shipwrecked (the accident was not always unexpected...). He contacted a firm in Valparaíso and Gastón Blanchard, one of the employees, went to work for him. His job consisted in coaching Nogueira on how to enter the business circles of Santiago de Chile. He introduced him to politicians and influential people who could give him a hand in the process of becoming a multiple entrepreneur. A few years later he had managed to lease approximately one million two hundred thousand hectares of land.

Nogueira and Blanchard became partners in the principal shipping and trading company of Punta Arenas.

José Nogueira went up in the world not only financially but also socially. That was when he realized that his first wife, Rose Peralta, who had staunchly backed him when he was just a sea-lion hunter and who was wonderful behind the counter in his store, didn't really fit in with the fashionable social circles in Chile.

His wife knew him well. She was fully aware of his fierce determination; when his mind was set on something nothing –and nobody- could deter him from achieving his goal. He was good at threats, too... Having all those facts in mind she agreed to divorce him, in exchange for a substantial sum of money.

And so Nogueira married –for the second and last time- Sara Braun. He had no children in either of his marriages.

José Menéndez came from a very humble family in Asturias. He was only a youngster when he traveled to Cuba where he worked as a shop assistant. Somehow he turned up in Buenos Aires, began working as an employee in a navy hardware store. He married the daughter of some French immigrants called María Behety. Shortly after his marriage and by request of the firm that employed him, he and his young wife had to travel to Punta Arenas.

Governor Oscar Viel was convinced that Luis Piedra Buena was an agent of the Argentine government. Therefore he denied him permission to continue operating his navy goods store. That brought about the commercial downfall of Piedra Buena in Punta Arenas, who became a dilatory debtor of Etchart y Cía. of Buenos Aires.

In 1876, José Menéndez went to Punta Arenas as the official collector of the above mentioned firm. After carefully studying the perspectives of the local market he decided to buy Piedra Buena's debt for a paltry sum of money. He grabbed at this unique opportunity and became owner of his first property.

Elías Braun and his family had settled in Punta Arenas in 1874. He, together with his wife, Sara and their children –Oscar and Mauricio- had escaped from a pogrom against the Jewish community, in Lithuania. They embarked at Hamburg, supposedly bound for Buenos Aires. They changed their minds, though, when they found out that the Chilean government had an interesting proposition to offer all immigrants who were willing to settle in Punta Arenas: a plot of land, some animals to start with, materials to build a house and sufficient supplies to meet their needs for six months.

Apart from exploiting the land he was given north of Punta Arenas, Elías Braun also installed a store and a small hotel.

In 1872, Oscar Viel, Governor of the Magellian territory, was informed that a foreign brig (the *Treponts*) had capsized in the Magellan Straits and that the crewmen had been attacked by natives of Tierra del Fuego. There were no warships anchored in Punta Arenas at the time; in fact, the only ships available belonged to sea-lion hunters or fishermen. Only an expert seaman could rescue the castaways. Consequently Viel had to swallow his pride, put away his chauvinist prejudices and send for Piedra Buena. He sent a messenger to the naval store –already in pretty bad shape-. His orders were to contact "Captain Luis" (the Argentine President Bartolomé Mitre had named him "honorary

Captain") and ask him to take on this salvage operation.

Piedra Buena accepted. His only condition was to be given "…an adequate vessel with all the necessary equipment" He also made it quite clear that he "was relinquishing the fees that anybody else in my place would charge".

Only one ship in the harbor met his requirements: the *"Rippling Wave"*.

One of the crewmen he took along on the *"Rippling Wave"* was Juan Caballero, a Tierra del Fuego Indian who had been brought up by Piedra Buena. During that voyage they encountered fierce gales and fearful storms. In fact, it figures as a remarkable naval prowess in the history of the Magellan Straits.

Captain Piedra Buena fulfilled his mission only to discover the remains of what appeared to be a demoniac orgy. First he came upon all that was left of the ship's captain: just bones, horrifying remnants of a cannibalistic feast. The other members of the crew had drowned while trying to escape from the Indians. When Captain Piedra Buena got a clear picture of the dreadful misfortune that had befallen the *"Treponts"´* crew he decided to go back. The return voyage was just as perilous as the first. The Captain was very worried because the wind beat furiously on the battered ship and tore the sails to shreds. In a last, desperate attempt to save the ship and his men, he managed to luff next to the coast. Thanks to that maneuver he not only avoided crashing against the rocks, it also ran the ship aground without the aid of an anchor or chains.

Going one step further, he chose the best men of the crew and sailed to Punta Arenas to seek help. The remaining men stayed behind with meager supplies (just a sack of beans) to wait for the ship that would come to their rescue. Only Piedra Buena could get across the Magellan Straits in the middle of a storm with just the help of some oars and the sad shreds of torn sails. Fortunately they were picked up by an English ship and taken to Punta Arenas, where "Captain Luis" quickly rigged a vessel and went to rescue the Rippling Wave and its crew.

When his mission was fulfilled, Piedra Buena went personally to see Governor Viel, to give him a full report of the events, return the schooner and inform him that the crew had returned safe and sound.

Another mutiny took place in 1877. This time it was the artillery men in cahoots with the convicts of the army prison, who committed all sorts of crimes. Murder, rape, looting, there was no limit to what these men could do, specially when they practically lived in a state of drunkenness and debauchery. They robbed the stores –including the one belonging to José Menéndez, who was away at the time- and destroyed the homes of terror-stricken villagers who fled the town. The governor, Duble Almeyda, was badly injured. Even so, he was able to escape and went for help to Skyring bay, where the war ship *"Magallanes"* was anchored.

A devastated land was the outcome of all this crazy subversive onslaught. Many families left Punta Arenas. Afraid lest all attempts to attract new inhabitants should fail, the government decided to close down the prison, whose inmates always outnumbered the guards by a long stretch.

José Menéndez was adamant that he would not be driven out by criminals. He set out to restore his financial situation by trading with the Tehuelches. Buying and selling guanaco hides, feathers and furs allowed him to stay in business while rebuilding his store.

The store belonging to Elías Braun was also ravaged but no personal harm came to any members of the family.

Coincidentally, the English farmer Henry Reynard brought to the Straits some three hundred sheep from Malvinas. That event brought about an important productive expansion in all the region, particularly in the Argentine south on account of its vast territory. The English textile industry became the principal consumer of local wool. That meant that somebody was going to get very rich. An explosive increase in production opened up a whole new panorama for both commerce and the naval industry. Somehow or other Nogueira, Braun and Menéndez became more and more successful in their new ventures. And they owned more and more lands.

Santa Cruz didn´t partake of the prosperity that was rapidly transforming all the southern territory of Chile: in 1882 it had a scant population, and the center of local activity was Piedra Buena´s store, on the island of Pavón. All attempts to attract new inhabitants had ended in failure.

The Brauns were taking all the necessary measures to take a solid stand in the local economic circles with the idea of, eventually, expanding across Patagonia. They managed vast extensions of land –around two million hectares- and the family assets were further increased when Mauricio took over the administration of the enormous fortune his sister Sara inherited when her husband –José Nogueira- died.

Braun and Blanchard (Nogueira´s ex partner) formed a new company -a shipping, commercial and industrial firm-, with subsidiaries in Puerto Santa Cruz and San Julián.

Mauricio Braun´s marriage to Josefina Menéndez Behety –José Menéndez´s eldest daughter- brought the two families even closer, thus favoring new joint ventures. Menéndez had also launched into an agricultural exploitation on a large scale and rounded up more than a million hectares (his first big operation had been the *estancia* San Gregorio, in the Strait, which enabled him to acquire another sixty thousand hectares in Tierra del Fuego) and had dealings with the shipping industry as well. He was the first to use coastal steamboats. He established subsidiaries in Río Gallegos and Santa Cruz.

Braun and Menéndez merged gradually. They shared the ownership of the Bank of Punta Arenas, - which afterwards changed its name to Banco de Chile y Argentina-. Together they undertook several new enterprises: mining, meatpacking and shipping companies, among other commercial concerns.

In the case of the Englishman William Greenwood, it was altogether a different story. This gentleman, who was 30 years old and came from a very distinguished family in York, had made a considerable sum of money trading in Punta Arenas. Unfortunately, he lost it all in some obscure financial operation. Greenwood was most disappointed with the commercial circles of Punta Arenas (which, in the opinion of the Argentine explorer Ramón Lista, reeked of dishonest merchants), gave up business and decided to go up north. He left the comfortable city life to mingle with hunters and Indians and explorers. He was not alone in this. Francisco Poivre, a Frenchman from Marseille who was also sick of the commercial greed of Punta Arenas, adhered to Greenwood´s idea of living in absolute freedom, no ties attached, and joined up with him.

Their association was based on a spiritual communion, not knowing yet what sort of activity was in store for them. They knew for certain that gold seeking did not interest them, and they definitely shunned anything connected with trade or commerce. Each had a horse, rifle, trappings and *boleadoras*, and that was their only capital.

They rode up north, passed through Ultima Esperanza, then flanked the cordillera and set up camp in a valley of incredible beauty. They were dazzled by the display of rare wild-flowers, the lenga forests and those enormous oaks – some were fifteen meters high-. A rustling sound excited their curiosity... it was a river just nearby, with rushing waters and strong currents. They didn´t hesitate, not for one second. They unsaddled the horses and set about building a log cabin on the river bank. They could wade through the river and there was good fishing as well. Greenwood named the river Turbio.

A few days later they went hunting, and on their return they came across lieutenant Juan Tomás Rogers, an English scientist who worked for the Chilean government. He was inspecting the river. He duly wrote in his report that he had chanced upon a mighty river "...which Mr. Greenwood named Turbio on account of its waters".

Rogers was an officer of the Chilean ship *"Magallanes"* and had been commissioned by his government to carry out a hydrographic survey. Which was precisely what he was up to when he met Greenwood and Poivre. He got a glimpse of the Cordillera de los Baguales -or Sierra de los Baguales- later known as Torres del Paine. Rogers described them as "irregular shaped" and with snowcapped peaks. The term "bagual" originates in the border zone between Argentina and Chile, where horses reproduced in large quantities within the area between the river Turbio and Lago Argentino. These horses had supposedly escaped from the Indians who camped at the foot of the mountain range.

In the opinion of the Argentine explorer Carlos M. Moyano these horses were not apt for labor because they tired easily. But in climbing up a steep slope they were unbeatable.

The wandering partners returned with a group of Tehuelches and a herd of horses. It hadn't been an easy task to lasso and break the horses, but our friends were quick to learn from the Indians all the tricks that would enable them to survive in the desert, to get acquainted with the paths and passes hitherto ignored by the white man and to discover secret watering places and grazing lands.

The instinct that led them to this unorthodox lifestyle had already dwelled in Darwin's thoughts: "There is great joy in the independence of the gaucho's way of life: it's the possibility of reining the horse in to a stop and say: we'll spend the night here". And regarding the gaucho's talent in interpreting the desert, he wrote: "Just one look at the trail and they know its history".

Greenwood and Poivre were tireless rovers, but every now and then they returned to the cabin by the river; they rode all along Lago Argentino, Punta Arenas, Río Gallegos, Puerto Santa Cruz, Viedma or Patagones and different sites of the cordillera.

Nobody who knew them could understand why these two refined, cultured men led such a rough, solitary existence in that uncivilized region, in close contact with the aborigines. They were on very friendly terms with the Indians, who quite willingly let them in on the secrets of the land and the tricks that were the basis of survival.

Sometimes they enjoyed the company of a Chilean called Santiago Zamora, who was a famous scout in those days. He went along with "the two gringos" on their jaunts and taught them many things about the region. Once they rode up to Planicies de Diana, from there to the bay Ultima Esperanza, across Santa Cruz until they reached river Gallegos, which they waded through a pass that lieutenant Rogers identified as Paso de los Robles. They used to hunt during these excursions and sold their prey (ostriches, foxes, pumas and guanacos) at the nearest town.

The Hourcadette excursion was the first to explore the southern part of the Hielo Continental. One of its members climbs an ice-covered peak.

An unusual view of Punta Arenas (1871) such as it appears in Robert O. Cunningham's book "Notes on the Natural History of the Strait of Magellan and West Coast of Patagonia".

Above: Cordillera de los Andes: La Casa de la Cumbre (The house at the top) watercolor painted by Brambila, in 1794.
Left: Araucanos returning to Chile with stolen cattle and women and children taken prisoner during one of their savage incursions in the pampas near Buenos Aires.

A convoy of cargo-mules loaded with merchandise to be exchanged on either side of the cordillera.
In the past, mules were the only means of transportation.

"El Cruce de los Andes". In this painting, Durand reconstructs a scene showing troops of San Martín's army halting to rest. (Museo Histórico Nacional de Buenos Aires).

Muleteers on an expedition, eating an asado.

Guillermo Greenwood, an English adventurer, collaborated with scientific expeditions and took part in survey explorations aimed to further the colonization of Santa Cruz. He was looked upon as a "bohemian globetrotter".

Edelmiro Mayer, Governor of Santa Cruz, led a very picturesque life: he fought in the army of the North during the U.S. Civil War and then, in Mexico, in Benito Juárez's forces. He distinguished himself with many acts of selfless heroism.

Above: Alberto M. De Agostini, Salesian priest, explorer and mountaineer, with Selknam Hallmink, an Indian Chief of the Ona Tribe of Tierra del Fuego, dressed in guanaco hides. DeAgostini explored all the patagonian and fueguian cordillera.

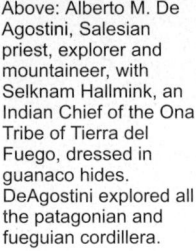

The German pioneer Hermann Eberhardt fought hard to overcome an adverse and demanding nature.

Gunther Plusschow explored the region on his D-1313 seaplane "Cóndor de Plata". He and his copilot Ernst Dreblow go over the flight plan before flying over the Hielo, where they both finally met their death.

The tenacity of Horacio Fisher know no bounds when it came to pursuing criminals throughout the Andes.

F. P. Moreno was the first to row a boat on Lake Traful.

The naturalist Clemente Onelli.

Sir Thomas Holdich, British arbitrator in the limits dispute between Argentina and Chile, in the company of Francisco P. Moreno, Clemente Onelli and other experts on an exploratory mission.

The Lively brothers pose with a native: although English by birth, they were registered as Argentine inhabitants during the limits dispute and later settled by Lake San Martín.

1916. The five members of the second expedition to Hielo Continental Patagónico: L. Witte, A. Kolliker, P. Tomsen, F. Kuhn and J. Jorgensen. They were sponsored by the German Scientific Society of Buenos Aires.

Members of the first expedition, "Comisión Flora Argentina" (1914): F. Reichert, C. M. Hicken, J. Jorgensen and L. Hauman

The Swiss Argentine Alfredo Kolliker and Lutz Witte.

Carlo Mauri was the first "Alpinist" to tackle the patagonian Andes, and he encouraged other Italian colleagues to follow his example and conquer the most difficult peaks. Mauri was a prominent mountaineer in the Alps, Patagonia and Asia, and carried out research tasks in major explorations.

The renowned French mountain-climber Lionel Terray preparing to set up camp at the foot of the Fitz Roy.

Argentine expedition to the Hielo Continental led by Emiliano Huerta (1953). Getting ready to camp.

Andreas Madsen loading cargo. An obliging man, he was always ready to give a hand and was the invaluable support in all expeditions. However, he made it quite clear that he did it "for love of God, not mountain-climbing".

The Dane Andreas Madsen lived in this idyllic place. He said: "This is the dream of the world of my childhood: a space that has no limits and lands without an owner". He chose the valley facing the Ftiz Roy (1902) for its beauty regardless of whether the land was apt for cattle-breeding. He grew rye, vegetables and fruit trees. His estancia, like one of his sons, was named Fitz Roy.

Footbridge across the Río de las Vueltas. In the background, the Cordón Adela, the Cerro Torre and the Fitz Roy.

An imposing view of the Torre. "Purists" consider Casimiro Ferrari was the first to conquer it, but others are convinced it was Maestri. Ferrari poses for Carlo Mauri shortly before reaching the summit.

Below left: sled on skis devised for the Kolliker expedition to the Hielo Continental.

Below right: The Fitz Roy in its towering magnificence, first conquered by French mountaineers.

Awestruck mountaineers face the imposing majesty of the Torre. The most famous peak of the patagonian Andes has always demanded the utmost effort from mountain-climbers of international fame.

A makeshift bridge made of tree-trunks over the Fitz Roy River.

Cesare Maestri (standing) and his team, showing the controversial compressor.

The Englishman Eric Shipton enjoyed exploring wild faraway places. He spent two years traveling all over Tierra del Fuego, and reached the Hielo Continental between 1958 and 1960.
Left: The challenge of climbing the Torre.

The Pascal Shelter on the edge of the Upsala Glacier.

Mountain-climbers are imbued with a feeling of absolute solitude and insignificance when faced with the Hielo Continental. The picture shows them groping their way along the crevices.

La Cristina Base, next to the Upsala glacier. This picture was taken in 1970 by members of the expedition sent by the Instituto del Hielo Continental.

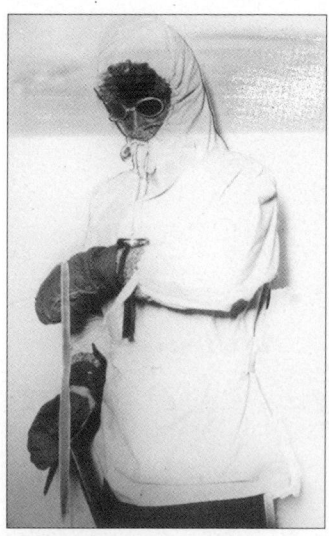

Adrienne Bance de Link returning to camp after a storm.

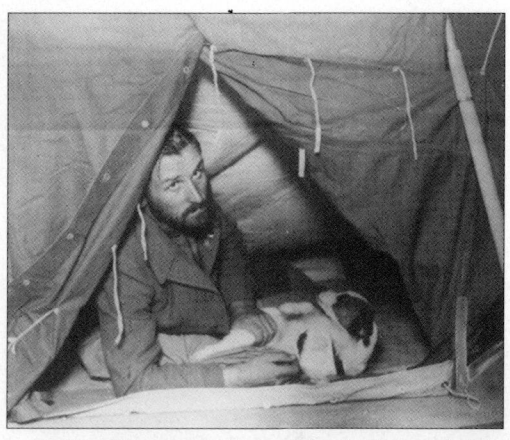

Hans George Link -known as the "solitary condor" for having climbed the Aconcagua on his own resting in the tent next to the dog "Fifi". The married couple became a romantic legend of the Aconcagua.

Mules were indispensable in the Andean territory.

Grave where the Links were buried, in the cemetery of Puente del Inca, situated in the Andes of Mendoza. They died when a violent storm caught them on their return from the summit of Aconcagua.

Different scenes in the Andes: animals carrying supplies to set up camp; a spectacular view of the Torre, near the summit; a team of explorers trudging westward on the Hielo Continental; mountaineers advancing slowly through the "white wind".

Route Nº 40 in one of its pebbly stretches, flanking the cordillera.

Another fascinating view of the Hielo Continental.

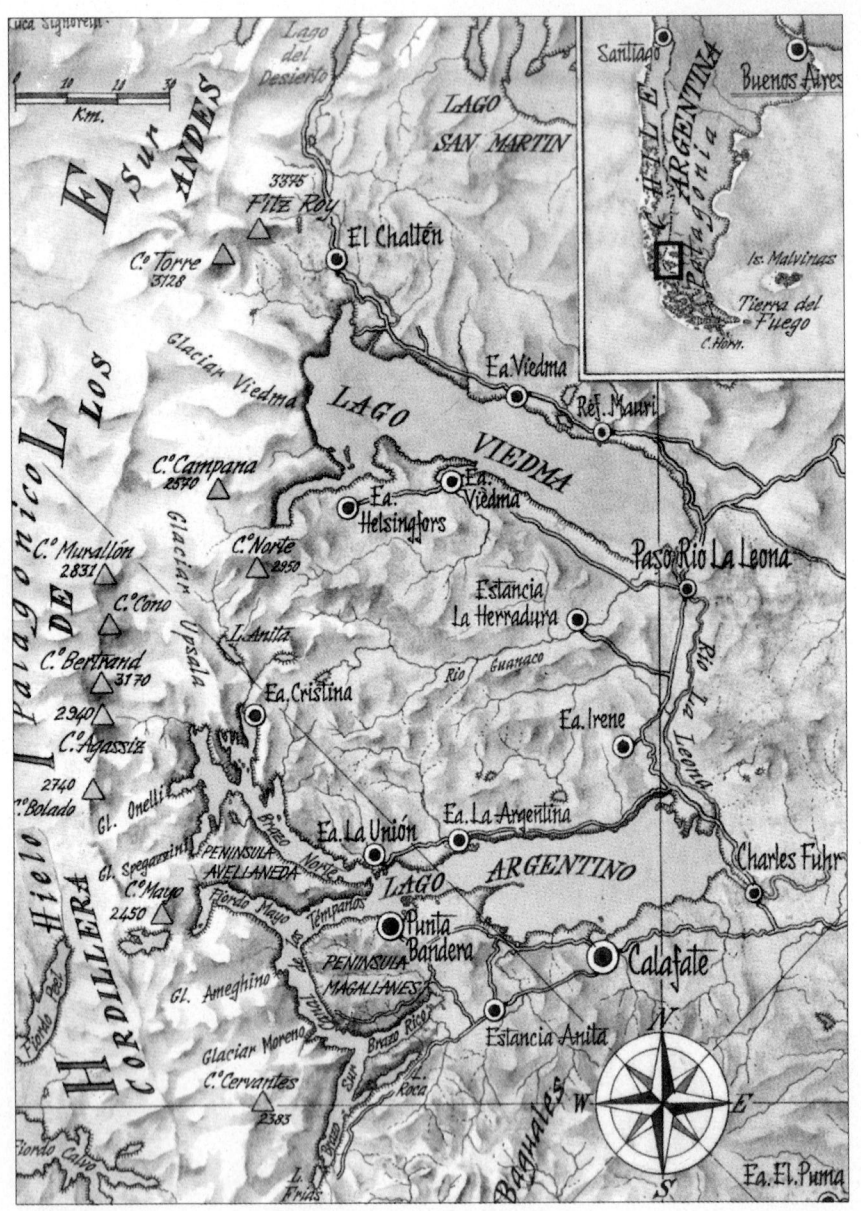

Map drawn by the Italian mountain climber Lucca Signorelli.

10.- THE EXPEDITION OF AGUSTIN DEL CASTILLO

A young sailor called Agustín del Castillo, who served the Argentine government, went on an expedition to the cordillera with the purpose of locating gold deposits and to make a survey of the land. He covered all the area surrounding Lake Argentino and reached the Turbio. Although he found no traces of gold, he did detect huge, rich coal seams. The same that Moreno, Moyano and Lista had predicted in previous explorations.

The Argentine President Domingo F. Sarmiento believed in the importance of coal mining and gave powerful impulse to its development. The law 448, which was proclaimed in 1870, instituted a 25.000 pesos reward for every person who discovered a coal mine that could be exploited at a profit.

In 1881, the explorer and scientist Francisco P. Moreno ("perito Moreno") was working in the Border Committee trying to establish the limits between Argentina and Chile. During his research he reported to the government that the coal stratum covered the area between the Magellan Strait and the northern part of Lake San Martín and that there was an enormous amount of wood in the region. His logical deduction was that mining population centers could be established all along the stretch from the plains of Diana to the Atlantic, and plenty of grazing lands for agricultural exploitation as well.

Agustín del Castillo disembarked in Río de Janeiro. In order to begin his hydrographic studies he needed tools and equipment that had to be sent from Buenos Aires. In the meantime, he was forced into an irritating inactivity which lasted for more than six months. He finally took off on his own; he was bound for the cordillera, urged by a "powerful enthusiasm for all that was connected with the soil".

Having heard that the manager of a mining company that exploited gold-bearing sands in Cabo Vírgenes was organizing an expedition to Lago Argentino, Agustín del Castillo went personally to see Nicolás Dávila (such was his name) and requested he be allowed to join it. After all, they were bound for the same place...

The nine members of the expedition were equipped with forty horses, three dogs, three tents, rifles, boxes of bullets, lassoes, *boleadoras* and enough food for three months. Most of the men were frustrated gold-seekers, but there were also herdsmen and the occasional romantic "Patagonian rover". The expedition advanced westward, coasting the River Chico.

All along the way del Castillo took notes of the topographic characteristics regarding vegetation and the river course. His final report was published by the Instituto Geográfico Argentino. Dávila was most helpful and provided him with whatever tools or equipment he needed for his research. They became quite friendly, went to hunt *chulengos* together and shared some tasty *asados*. Sometimes they even slept in a guanaco habitat; these animals sleep in holes filled with layers of loose soil which felt rather like a mattress. Very early one morning they were woken by a heavy downpour and they left in a hurry, carrying their saddles on their backs. They didn´t know where to go exactly, they roamed at random until they reached a Tehuelche camp. Ignacio, the Indian Chief, gave them a warm welcome and provided them with some leather garments while their own clothes were set to dry. They were also invited to eat plentiful *asados* of ostrich, puma and guanaco meat.

A young girl whose face was daubed with bright colors invited them with mate: it was prepared in a large container with a long, peculiar shaped *bombilla*. That was the typical Indian mate which could be made to last up to four hours even though it was made with a small amount of *yerba*,. The reason was that the white merchants who provided *yerba* to the Indians demanded an exorbitant price for it.

Del Castillo was fascinated by the Tehuelches: he carefully registered all their moves and wrote detailed accounts of their behavior, customs, the way they dressed, how they talked and expressed themselves, their gestures and reactions.

All the Indian families approached the strangers to pay their respects. The guests were deeply touched by the way the Tehuelche community greeted them.

They remained in the camp until the rain stopped. During all that time they indulged in unending *asados*, and resignedly drank the equally unending, watery mates, being always careful to express their gratitude for the generous hospitality shown to them by the Tehuelches. During the night they slept comfortably wrapped in warm *quillangos*.

The Tehuelches enjoyed their new friends´ company. The young girls dressed up like for an important festivity: they wore their finest clothes and beads and adorned their hair with colored ribbons.

The two men were impressed at the Tehuelche´s respect for family ties, and their protective care for orphans and old people who had no family to look after them. One detail made them aware of this particular trait, which was when two Indians interrupted a journey and retraced the hundred and fifty kilometers´ distance just to bring back a horse that had been lost by an orphan of the Indian camp. They just rested awhile and then left as if it were nothing at all.

"I met an Indian called Peso Grande –wrote del Castillo- who had once been very rich and his fortune was now reduced to one lame horse, the reason being that almost all his children had died and he´d had to sacrifice the animals he owned. Now he pays his tribute to *Cacique* Ignacio".

Other characteristics of the Tehuelche idiosyncrasy also intrigued our young explorer, as, for instance, the fact that they upheld their superstitious beliefs even if it meant going against their own interests. Also, he couldn´t understand why they never imitated the white man in his efforts to protect his belongings. Why, being so poor, they insisted on sacrificing the horses that had belonged to a dead son, thus enforcing their own poverty.

The day came when it was time to leave. The Tehuelches begged their friends to stay on so they could attend the initiation ceremony of two young girls. Considering they had been so well attended, the travelers graciously accepted the invitation and stayed on for a couple of days.

The celebration began with monotonous, sad songs; then they lit bonfires to roast horse meat; at midday they started sacrificing mares and the blood was poured into large bowls that were passed around until everybody had inhaled its smell. They continued eating and dancing throughout the afternoon, a musical group beat on primitive drums while the men danced around in a circle, and the party went on and on...

Next morning, after Ignacio and his people bade them farewell, the group resumed its journey towards the cordillera.

Agustín del Castillo was aware of the gradual decay of the aboriginal ethnic, and gave a word of warning: "The state of poverty is pitiful... its causes being the scarcity of hunting game and the vile commerce carried out by mobs of Chilean tradesmen –from Punta Arenas- who, aided by a few bottles of poisoned liquor, prepare the ground for their lucrative business".

They traveled non-stop for fourteen days until they got a glimpse of the Sierras Baguales; during the crossing of a small lake they were fiercely attacked by horseflies and mosquitoes, forcing them to take a rest and nurse the nasty bumps that covered their faces and arms.

On the following afternoon they finally got to the foot of the Sierras Baguales, surrounded by herds of guanacos that ran in all directions. It was quite a show. The peones chased the animals as a kind of game or entertainment, but also with hopes of capturing wild horses.

At one point the expedition split up: del Castillo was bound southwards, towards Ultima Esperanza, and Dávila had to go up north, to Lago Argentino. Dávila gave the young sailor twelve horses, two peones, a dog and a tent. Then they shared an *asado*. Few words were spoken. With a heavy heart, both friends embraced, then each went his own way...

The following morning, del Castillo made a stop next to a stream, Las Vizcachas, then continued until he reached the foot of the Paine where he made a careful survey of his surroundings; after that he traveled to Laguna Azul. While he carried out his customary reconnaissance task the peones went fishing. They caught some magnificent specimens, which they enjoyed eating in the evenings, sitting around the fire.

The group bordered a river course and reached a place called Corral de Zamora, which belonged to a Chilean native considered the best *baquiano* (scout) that ever crossed the southern part of the cordillera. He was well-known in all the south of Chile, in fact, he was a sort of legend. He appeared to be gruff, rather hostile and very much of a loner. However, a few drinks operated a kind of magic turning him into an emotional person with a definite touch of fanaticism. This was especially noticeable every September 18th, when he celebrated the anniversary of the Chilean Independence.

Apart from the Indians, with whom he held a close relationship, he was known to have only two other friends: Greenwood and Poivre. The three had gone on long journeys throughout the south of Chile, the Andes and southern Patagonia. He knew every nook and cranny of the cordillera like nobody else did, and earned his two gringo friends´ fervent admiration, not only for his scouting skills but also for his courage, which became evident on several occasions. Like the time he escaped from an ambush set by ferocious horse thieves who were after the horses he and his friends were herding with the purpose of selling them to a Chilean dealer. Zamora "did away with two of them, and the gringos one each". One of the criminals escaped although he had been badly wounded by a stroke of Zamora´s knife, which proved that he was as deft with a knife as he was with a rifle.

However, age didn´t agree with him... as he grew older he became more grumpy and unsociable.

Del Castillo was sickened when he approached Zamora and was hit by the nauseating smell that emanated from his body scarcely covered in filthy rags, and the grime that blackened his hovel; he was surrounded by around twenty dogs that scratched in despair and shook wildly, kicking up clouds of dust.

Del Castillo wrote in his report: "...he´s lost his memory and suffers all kinds of ailments brought about by old age. He´s become impertinent and insufferable... this man used to be a kind of working machine, he alone captured hundreds of wild cows and mares and was considered the best lasso in the territory. His name figures in almost every legend and anecdote of Patagonia".

Del Castillo finally offered to send some peones who could provide him with game and fish, but Zamora bluntly refused. He grudgingly accepted packages of yerba and salt, because he hadn´t had salt for more than a year...

Agustín del Castillo carried on with his research in the vicinity of the cordillera. From the top of a mountain he saw a beautiful lake he didn´t know existed, and promptly decided to set up camp on its shores.

The expedition made a stop to rest and make an *asado*. While they were lighting the fire, they perceived at a distance the figure of a rider emerging from the grasslands.

The stranger approached on horseback and raised his hat in salute. It was Guillermo Greenwood, who was later invited by del Castillo to join their expedition.

About that lake that so intrigued del Castillo, Greenwood said its name was "Toro", on account of its having been for a long time the favorite grazing place of a very large, white, wild bull that no hunter had, as yet, been able to bring down; both Indians and hunters alike shared a superstitious belief that this animal was invincible.

Nevertheless, the year before Greenwood and Poivre had been attacked by the bull and they shot it dead. The Englishman also told Agustín del Castillo that during the five years of adventurous roaming he had never gone further than the River Turbio and the Bay Ultima Esperanza. Still, he willingly accepted to join the group and scout for them. He only asked to have a few days so that he could look for Poivre and ask him to join the expedition as well. As from that day, del Castillo and Greenwood had a warm, friendly relationship.

Poivre was a most interesting personality, held in high esteem by all those who knew him –as I described in "Patagonia, History, Myths and Legends"-. He collected feathers and quillangos and was most helpful with the Albarracín couple who had settled down in the desert territory of Santa Cruz at the worst possible moment. As María Salomé de Albarracín wrote in her memoirs: "The only profit we ever made was buying feathers and quillangos from the Indians and then selling them to old Poivre". Francisco Poivre was the only person who helped Mrs. Albarracín in childbirth, because her husband hadn´t been able to make it from Misioneros in time.

Quite near Valle de la Pintura, with its ochre, clay soil that the Indians used for their paintings, there is a 1.800 meters high mountain that stands out by itself in the desolate steppes. It was named El Gorro de Poivre (Poivre´s Cap) in honor of this adventurer who roamed this place which, according to the naturalist Clemente Onelli, was "the Creator´s largest oversight on earth".

Poivre didn´t have his partner´s charm nor his imposing personality. Of course he was quite a bit older and that maybe accounted for his reserved nature. He felt quite at ease in the solitary surroundings they chose to live in and, in fact, handled all the situations that arose in this rough environment with the same cleverness and audacity as his English friend. Whenever his silhouette disappeared into the morning mist to get back to the desert, he left behind him a kind of melancholy feeling, and there was something definitely enigmatic about him.

But there was no doubt that both learnt to overcome the desert, they acquired an intimate knowledge of the land and its lakes, they penetrated the heart of the mountain range which held no secrets from them.

When Greenwood and Poivre met Agustín del Castillo at the riverside of the Turbio they traveled together towards the attractive salt-water bay called Ultima Esperanza. And from there on to the Bay Obstrucción. They hadn´t eaten for at least two days, so they went hunting for their dinner before getting down to their reconnaissance job.

Agustín del Castillo thought the time had come to hoist the Argentine flag. To that purpose he chose a place which was very near the location where Puerto Natales would later be founded. First they climbed a mountain, pulled down a couple of trees and used the logs to assemble a tripod and a wooden pole; then he drew up a deed which was duly signed by the three men. Finally, he put the document inside a bottle which they buried at the foot of the tripod.

The two tough, weather-beaten older men felt deeply moved by the enthusiasm of young del Castillo who held the flag in his arms and spoke in a tremulous, rather solemn voice. These were his words:

"My friends. You have come along with me all this way in a totally disinterested fashion, with keen enthusiasm and a most generous disposition. From the bottom of my heart I thank you for your care and devotion and I hope someday my country will also show its gratitude to you.

The moment has come when I will ask you to accompany me once more in honoring this flag which is not your flag but it does protect many of your fellow-countrymen who live freely and happily in its comforting shade. England and France are so full of glory that no French or English citizen can possibly feel jealous because of this small act with which I honor my country".

After having delivered his brief and very heartfelt speech, del Castillo began to hoist the flag amid the fervent "Hurras!!" of the two hunters who wanted to join their young friend in this moment of solemn fervor.

Of course, these two veteran scouts felt rather embarrassed by this display of emotions and meaningful words. But the affection they felt for this young man was much stronger than their natural reticence and they patted his back and shook his hand in a show of comradeship.

A few weeks later they reached Río Gallegos. This last journey had been exhausting and they were all in very bad shape. It was almost a year now that del Castillo had been sleeping out in the open.

Del Castillo finished his report to Minister Racedo with one last suggestion: "I particularly request that Your Excellency give special consideration to the valuable services rendered to me voluntarily and with no personal interest of any kind, by the Patagonian inhabitants Messrs. Guillermo Greenwood and Francisco Poivre, who joined my expedition, providing me with elements I lacked and contributing to the successful achievement of its purpose".

Agustín del Castillo felt deep gratitude towards those two men who had generously offered to help in his explorations and research, and made a point of paying them a visit whenever he had the time and the means to do so. Unfortunately, he died shortly after of "lung apoplexy", or so it figured in his death certificate.

He was then only 34 years of age.

11.- FIGHTING FOR A GOOD CAUSE

Edelmiro Mayer was Ramón Lista´s successor as Governor of Santa Cruz. Both men shared the same ideal, which was to attract inhabitants and to further the development and progress of the southern region. This was no small challenge considering the extension of this bare territory where there was everything to be done.

He was another Patagonian pioneer.

Edelmiro Mayer was born in Buenos Aires in 1837. His father was an Englishman called John Andrew Mayer Arnold and his mother was Doña Dolores Posadas.

Although he was a gifted scholar in mathematics, he abandoned his studies to join the army as Second Lieutenant of Artillery during the war against the Confederacy; later he was made an officer of the Frontier Army, where he collaborated with Bartolomé Mitre.

He was very much in love with a young *Porteña* and wanted to marry her. But the girl´s parents, who were partial to the dictator Juan Manuel de Rosas, opposed this marriage for political reasons. Mayer was very disappointed and decided to go to the United States, where he stayed for eight years.

When the Civil War broke out he declared himself against slavery and offered to fight for the army of the North. Owing to his knowledge and specific training he was made an Infantry Captain. He organized a regiment of colored soldiers and obtained remarkable victories on the battlefields.

Due to his outstanding performance he was promoted to Lieutenant Coronel. General Grant, who had heard of his expertise and heroism requested to meet him personally. After the interview, he was named one of the General´s immediate collaborators. His first assignment was to assist President Lincoln, with whom he stayed until the day of the murder.

He had great admiration for Lincoln and was grief-stricken by his tragic death, which led him to eventually leave the North American army. From there he went to Mexico and joined the forces of Benito Juárez who fought against the French army that upheld the emperor Maximilian.

As it couldn´t be otherwise, his performance in the Mexican army was brilliant –especially in Querétaro- and he was soon promoted to General. During the time he fought alongside Porfirio Díaz he became involved in an unsuccessful uprising. His name was, in fact, on the list of prisoners with a death sentence and barely escaped being executed thanks to the timely intervention of the Argentine Ambassador in the United States, Domingo Faustino Sarmiento, who saved him on the condition that he would not return to Mexico.

He finally decided to go to London.

During his stay in the United Kingdom he became very friendly with Máximo Terrero and his wife, Manuelita Rosas. The young couple filled him with contradictory feelings: on one hand, he enjoyed their company. On the other hand, they made him feel conscious of all he lacked regarding his emotional life. He was still in love with the girl he had been forced to part with, and therefore decided to give his marriage plans another chance. He returned to Buenos Aires, firmly resolved to look for his love. Unfortunately, she had died a few months before...

Feeling depressed and eager to get away from Buenos Aires, he once again joined the army with the rank of General. Maybe he toyed with the idea of being transferred, but he soon discovered he no longer felt at ease in the army, and applied for retirement. Two years later he was elected as a congressman and when his period as a legislator was up he worked in different activities, alternating between journalist, translator and Director of the Western Railway. He even tried his luck as a builder.

He happened to meet Carlos Pellegrini when he was president of the Republic. Pellegrini sized him up and, after giving careful consideration to this man´s assets and know-how, he decided on him as the perfect candidate to succeed Ramón Lista in the governorship of Santa Cruz.

Mayer reached Río Gallegos just when the government house had burnt down in a fire. The Fentons lent him a house so that he could establish himself and begin his activity as Governor. His priority was to attract new inhabitants. He worked hard to achieve this goal and, in time, managed to establish settlers in Río Turbio, Planicies de Diana and Cancha Carrera.

He then met the overseas captain Hermann Eberhardt, definitely a man after his own heart.

When this German captain traveled to Buenos Aires he went directly to the Dirección de Tierras (Land Bureau) and said he was interested in acquiring land to colonize Chimen Aike: "...in an extension equivalent to the value of 1.000 pounds". That was the money he had.

The experiences these two men lived through are apparently quite dissimilar. However, they both ran similar risks.

When Eberhardt ventured on a month-long journey exploring the canals during a terribly harsh winter, it was more a dangerous challenge than an adventure. He left Punta Arenas in a small boat and sailed along the Worsley Canal and its branches Ultima Esperanza and Obstrucción. The landscape fascinated him, and the storms and blizzards he had to put up with didn´t stop him from pursuing a detailed survey of all the canals he came across. He anchored in a sheltered bay which he named Puerto Consuelo and completed the journey by land up to Río Turbio. He named the mountain Dorotea in memory of one of his daughters.

Seemingly, this lively captain of the merchant navy had found his place in the world. In Patagonia, right next to the Andes.

Following the tradition of families that descended from military Prussians, he was a cadet in the Military School. It didn´t take him long to break the tradition, though. He committed a serious breach of the school discipline and was judged by a Court whose president was no other than his very strict father. He carried out his punishment and then promptly put an end to his military career.

In Hamburg, young Eberhardt was on the loose and looking for some sort of job that would allow him to get away. Eventually he managed to get himself hired on a freighter and that´s how he landed in Alaska. He tried his luck in different activities, starting out as a gold-seeker, then as a hunter, and later as a laborer in a sawmill. Finally, he was taken on as a crew member on a whaler. He never lasted very long on a ship, these temporary jobs were really his way of getting around the world and seeing new places. He disembarked in China where he dabbled in commerce, and shortly after traveled to Manila, where he chose to fight with the Philippines against the Spanish occupation. Then he returned to Germany, where he was appointed First Officer in an overseas shipping line. During one of his travels, destination the Malvinas Islands, he suddenly decided to stay on terra firma and thus, his role as First Officer came to an abrupt end.

When he was definitely installed in the islands he served as coastal pilot in the same German shipping line where he had previously been First Officer and also in other British companies; he gradually expanded his activity to Tierra del Fuego and the Magellan zone, and he became the most skilled and sought-after coastal pilot in the southern region.

On board a transatlantic ship that was bound for Antofagasta he met a young girl –Margarita Wappler- who was going to work as a governess for a German family. When the ship left Valparaíso the two young people bade each other a sad farewell. Halfway through the voyage, Margarita´s sad expression gave way to a look of firm determination. Now that her mind was made up she eagerly looked forward to the next port, where she intended to disembark and go back to Punta Arenas. From there she would go to Malvinas, for the simple reason that she was determined to marry Eberhardt. Of course she asked after him in the shipping office, was he there, or maybe in town, when was he coming back, were they expecting him soon?, etc. etc.... In view of the fact that nobody seemed to know Eberhardt´s whereabouts, she boarded a ship that would take her to the islands.

They named their first daughter Dorotea.

Shortly after, a very rich Englishman of the nobility called Lord Dudley –ex Viceroy of India- crossed the southern region in his yacht *"Star of India"* during a pleasure cruise around the world. Eberhardt was contracted as coastal pilot and sailed from Montevideo to Valparaíso. During a stop in Río Gallegos he accompanied Lord Dudley on an ostrich-hunting excursion. They got as far as Chimen Aike. And, in the same way as Margarita Wappler, when she set eyes on Hermann exclaimed "This is my man!", when Eberhardt discovered Chimen Aike he proclaimed "This is my place!".

Once in Valparaíso Lord Dudley gave Eberhardt an envelope, paying him for services rendered. There were one thousand pounds in that envelope...precisely the money with which he bought his land at the Land Bureau.

He and his family moved to Chimen Aike taking some sheep with them. During the few months it took them to build their new home they became very friendly with the *Tehuelches* of a nearby camp. The natives proved to be excellent hosts and serviceable neighbors.

The Indians adored the charming little Dorotea. There is a picture taken of the little girl with long, golden curls, in the company of very solemn-looking *Tehuelches* staring fixedly at the strange machine that would immobilize them on a piece of paper.

During a visit to Rio Gallegos, Eberhardt introduced two acquaintances of his to Mayer: one was his cousin, Ernst von Heinz, and the other was Curt Meyer. The Governor gave twenty thousand hectares in the outskirts of Río

Turbio to each one on a provisional basis.

Curt Meyer founded the estancia "Rospentek". Heinz installed himself on the opposite margin, on land he named "Nueva Silesia", which later became the estancia "La Fermina" when Heinz decided to move up north to the estancia Tapí Aike.

Like all pioneers, nothing came easily to Curt Meyer. He worked very hard and had to overcome countless obstacles in order to succeed in the goals he had set himself. He personally cut the wood to build his house and yard and carried the stones from the river banks. He launched local sheep-breeding with the few animals Eberhardt had given him. He also had some hares sent from Germany. These quickly reproduced and brought forth specimens similar to the Patagonian hares only smaller in size.

Curt Meyer loved animals: the guanacos, *huemules*, gray foxes, ostriches, flamingoes and different species of pheasants and quails he imported from Europe, all led a peaceful coexistence in his valley. New species introduced by him –wild turkeys and turtledoves, among others- were welcome assets to the typical southern fauna, composed mainly of magellan thrushes, goldfinches, *bandurrias* and ducks. In the garden at the rear of his house he planted so many trees that in no time it became an impenetrable forest.

He staunchly put up with the scourges of an environment that was harsh and relentless. Snowstorms, blizzards, unending ice-cold rain, freezing cold or blazing heat... But the greatest menace was undoubtedly the puma, that threatened to do away with his herd of sheep.

In times of difficulties and privations it was quite customary to refer to the courageous actions of brave settlers as acts of heroism that would serve as an example to all those facing extreme situations. In a way, it was comforting to know that somebody else had gone through the same hardships and had been able to overcome them.

One of these anecdotes refers to Pablo Lenzner in the year 1889, during a terrible snowstorm that had blocked all roads. Something had to be done about it because he urgently needed to get to Río Gallegos to buy provisions and medicine. So he rigged up a makeshift sled and trained the sheepdogs to pull it. He totaled around three hundred and fifty kilometers going to Rio Gallegos and back under the raging snowstorm, solving problems as they arose, with spirit and quick reflexes. His neighbors were stunned. Nobody had, as yet, been able to triumph over a snow blockade. But then, there´s always a first time...

The settlers of neighboring districts got together when it was the time for sheep-shearing and the earmarking of livestock. Among them were Meyer, von Heinz, Wohler, Kart and the two Smith brothers, two Englishmen who eventually settled in California. As they lacked proper barns to gather the animals in, the colonists used to move from one camp to another improvising corrals with poles, lengths of rope, tree trunks, hides and rags. The bales of wool were then transported to Río Gallegos in oxcarts. Those journeys were slow-going and could last many days, even weeks. It was only when oxen were replaced by horses that transportation became faster and more efficient.

In 1896 a Survey Committee began taking measurements on Curt Meyer's land. The colonist was outraged when he found out the real reason behind those proceedings. Apparently, his lands formed part of a one-million-hectare extension that the State had sold to a certain Adolfo Grümbein who, in turn, was negotiating their sale to the Bank of Antwerp. The central government had voted in favor of the operation with Grümbein and cancelled the permission formerly given to the government of Santa Cruz for the granting of lands.

Mauricio Braun was most interested in expanding even further in Argentine territory. He was quick to grasp the general situation and promptly bought twenty thousand hectares from Grümbein. Thanks to valuable contacts he had in political circles, he was able to wangle a grant for the remaining lands, logically much larger than the one he paid for. In all these matters there was a sort of generally accepted trick: whenever a petitioner's claim exceeded a reasonable limit, that's when the "front men" appeared on the scene. They bought lands in their own names for the landowners who could not officially increase their possessions.

At the time, José Menéndez –Braun's father-in-law- lodged a complaint against the Salesian missionaries of Río Grande for protecting the Indians who stole sheep from his *estancias*. He made a point of discrediting their activity as missionaries, and objected to the contribution of one pound per Fueguian Indian that the Salesians demanded from the *estancieros* for every native they housed in their convents.

Father Fagnano replied: "...this question of the pound sterling arouses certain memories that make me wish to draw back the veil that covers them". He was alluding to the Indian-hunters who were paid by the *estancieros* one pound for every Indian they killed.

"El Diario" of Buenos Aires, in June 1899, published a statement of Menéndez in defense of J. Mac Lennan ("Chancho Colorado"), the manager of the estancia "Primera Argentina" who was well-known as an exterminator of Indians. He demanded that Fagnano retract his words and admit that the Mission was a hiding-place for Indian thieves. Otherwise he would be obliged to disclose "what he kept in reserve".

Instead of taking back his words —which was what Menéndez intended him to do- the Salesian priest went even further. He refuted Menéndez and promised to disclose the other four written pages he had in safe keeping. The Government and Church authorities in Buenos Aires intervened to put an end to a controversy that was threatening to disclose events of a very "delicate" nature that would demand positive action and investigations on the part of the government.

Curt Meyer discovered that the Governor of Santa Cruz´s actions to obtain a permanent grant of their lands for the settlers of Río Turbio had had negative results. Meyer stressed the fact that he was not demanding more land, just that which he already had.

Governor Mayer had received no information regarding the proceedings and the red tape involved. He was only informed that the sale of lands to Grümbein was a fait accompli and had been approved by the Senate.

Had the Government and Congress remained neutral in certain situations, Patagonia might have been less hit by adversity.

Eberhardt abandoned his lands in Los Morros and so did all the other settlers whose permits were on a provisional basis. They left even though their lands showed the improvements brought about by years of hard work.

But Curt Meyer never gave up, he never left his land because he felt they belonged to each other. It may be assumed that it wasn´t the idea of becoming rich that drove him to prosper, but rather the pleasure of seeing his beloved Rostenpek turn into his own private paradise.

He said the only way they could get him out of there was over his dead body. The inscription on a gravestone just a few yards from his cabin bears witness to that. It says: Curt Meyer – Died 20-3-1911.

And as to Ernst von Heinz, when he was out looking for land where he could settle on a —he hoped- permanent basis, he chanced upon an enormous hide and bones of what he thought was a prehistoric animal, inside a cave. He immediately got in touch with the Museum of La Plata. As a result they were able to reconstruct the mylodon, a prehistoric animal of Patagonia.

On December 24th 1911, Hermann Eberhardt, together with a group of German settlers, founded a colony in Chile, just a few kilometers away from Río Turbio. Owing to the date of its foundation (Christmas) it was named Puerto Natales. This became a prosperous cattle-breeding region, and a few years later two meat-packing establishments were inaugurated.

The few inhabitants along the cordillera in the territory of Santa Cruz were scattered very far from one another. Don Guillermo Payne, who arrived in Punta Arenas in 1896, moved to Lago Argentino in 1906 and chose to stay there permanently. The original population had settled at the foot of the mountain called Buenos Aires. By then only two inhabitants remained: the Englishmen Ernesto Cattle and Alfredo Game. They too left the region later on. Only Guillermo Payne stayed on in this incredibly beautiful and lonely place.

Percival Masters was born in Southampton. He was a sailor until he came to Patagonia, in 1900, when he abandoned his former occupation and became a tough, vigorous farmer and cattle-man. Together with his wife, Masters decided to go ahead with a project in a secluded place of Lago Argentino. They founded an establishment they called "La Cristina" in memory of one of their daughters who had died prematurely.

"La Cristina" became the regular stop for all expeditions traveling from the Upsala Glacier towards the Hielo Patagónico Sur.

12.- "A GROUP OF CHOSEN MEN"

The explorers, technicians and scientists who took part in the surveys that led to the demarcation of borders carried out their task regardless of the enormous sacrifices involved. Sometimes their assignments drove them to situations of risk. Such was the case when they ventured into regions hitherto unexplored and exposed their lives to unknown dangers. Clemente Onelli described these men as "a group of chosen men who had learnt to live by the rules of austerity and hardships". Men who felt awe and reverence for the distant, often inaccessible Patagonian territory.

Clemente Onelli was an Italian naturalist. After graduating in Rome he traveled to Argentina to work with the "perito" Moreno in the demarcation of borders; he later became Director of the Zoological Gardens in Buenos Aires. He died in this city in 1924.

Clemente Onelli carried out a thorough exploration of the Perito Moreno Glacier. In 1924 he reached the summit which was, in his opinion, the place where the real border was situated. The boundary was right there, in the part of the snowcapped cordillera "where passes narrow and trees become dwarf shrubs. Weeds and thorns disappear and the ground exudes water like a water-soaked sponge". Clemente Onelli described at length the difficulty of carrying the 300 kilos of iron to assemble the actual boundary device. The mules were unable to reach the top, so it was up to the men to carry the heavy load and the equipment, climbing their way up inch by inch, with the aid of an axe or a machete. He also mentioned the rainy season, when the damp and the cold seized the men´s bones and all they could dream of was a warm fire where they could recapture the feeling of blood running through their veins. However, the idea of a fire was usually wishful thinking. It could take hours to rake up some measly flames with wood that was always damp because of the rain or the water that oozed from the ground.

Both the "perito" Moreno and Clemente Onelli believed in the importance of attracting new inhabitants to settle in the, as yet, unpopulated Argentine lands, precisely at the moment when the Border Committee was demarcating the limiting boundary with Chile. On Moreno´s advice and Onelli´s insistence, the Englishman Gerald Lively and his two brothers, Hugh Robert and Joseph Percy, settled on the south coast of Lake San Martín. Gerald had fought in the Anglo-Boer war. He was an adventure-loving rover and had been living for some time in Tres Pasos, Ultima Esperanza. This place must have failed to meet his expectations because he readily accepted to move to the Lake San Martín district. He knew the area very well due to his frequent hunting expeditions. He also scouted for a group of English officers which carried out reconnaissance tasks around the lake. Leading this group was Colonel Holdich, the English arbitrator who had been assigned the demarcation of borders.

At the time Moreno was very worried because a group of engineers had been sent by Chile on a formal mission to claim the entire lake and the only inhabitants settled there were Chileans. That decided him to coax the Lively brothers to occupy those lands, in exchange for which he vouchsafed their ownership of the land if Argentine sovereignty was officially acknowledged.

Consequently, they proceeded to sell their belongings in Tres Pasos and buy more cattle for their new establishment. After traveling seven hundred kilometers they finally settled on the south coast of the lake.

Gerald Lively had high regard for both the "perito" Moreno and Clemente Onelli, and that must surely have been a strong motive behind the three brothers´ decision to become Argentine inhabitants. Owing to Gerald´s scouting skills he had earned a reputation as a reliable and trustworthy member of the English delegation. The officers told him the situation was bad enough due to the lack of Argentine inhabitants and was further aggravated by the Argentine authorities who had abandoned the location. To make matters worse, the Chileans had carried out an intense topographic task over the years, putting their local names on every mountain, site or stream they came across.

Lake San Martín was what Moreno found most fascinating. He wrote: "Civilization still ignores the existence of this lake; we must give it a name that will sponsor its progress... We shall call it San Martín, because its waters bathe the solid base of the Andes which is the only pedestal worthy of bearing the great warrior´s heroic image".

Moreno was aware of a sort of phony progress in Argentina, and he said as much to the Minister of Agriculture E. Ramos Mejía: "The only bustling movement to be seen is in the vicinity of the ports, which can be considered pieces of Europe. The rest of the country is often abandoned to its own resources".

During the fall, an English committee took upon itself the task of carrying out a reconnaissance campaign. Its members were the Captains Thomson and Robertson, a few Argentine technicians and a couple of sailors who were in charge of two canvas boats carried by mules. Knowing that the time of year was not apt for this kind of excursion, Gerald Lively earnestly advised the committee to postpone it. They set forth on their expedition anyway, regardless of his warning. That decision motivated Gerald Lively to write a scathing note in his diary: "I guess it will be an unforgettable experience for Robertson if we have bad weather".

However, the weather was fine and the passes free of snow. The Englishmen dedicated a great part of their time to hunting guanacos, ostriches, pumas and *huemules*.

They reached Lake Argentino and climbed Mt. Frías (1080 mts.). They took measurements and Gerald Lively wrote: "Robertson said to the Chileans that their maps were worthless".

They advanced eastward by the southern coast of the lake and crossed the Leona River two days later. They continued on their way coasting the east side of the Viedma and reached the valley of Chalía. By that time it had got very cold. They camped beside Lake Tar to rest and to update the maps and keep a record of all their notes. They found a note at the foot of a white flag. It was from Onelli, informing them that he had left all the provisions on the east coast of Lake San Martín.

On reaching Arroyo Calafate, Gerald saw two young bulls peacefully grazing at a distance. Next thing he knew there was some shooting, and shortly after the two English captains and Alvarez, the Argentine engineer, approached and informed him they had hit two "wild bulls", but that one of them had a bell hanging from his neck.

When the owner of the bulls –a German settler called Santiago Frank- reached the camp, the animals had already been slaughtered and hung from a couple of hooks. The foreigners made the formal introductions and explained the motive that drove them to that region. After which, there was nothing Frank could do except join them to share the *asado*. The only "souvenir" he recovered was the cowbell.

The mission then proceeded to Lake Belgrano, which was described by Gerald Lively in his diary as the most beautiful lake he had ever set eyes on. They carried out topographic tasks in these majestic surroundings. According to Gerald Lively, "it was like leafing through the great album of bygone ages. Life couldn´t be more pleasant, always providing the weather is good. Both Captains (Robertson and Thomson), sit next to the fire drinking a cup of hot toddy after a five-course meal. Of course, I´m sure they will recount to their friends in London all the hardships they went through in the Andes".

They resumed their journey, stopping every now and then to hunt *huemules*, or foxes. On one of these halts Gerald wrote in his diary: "It´s a pity the Argentine Government does nothing about these vast lands where there is space for millions of animals; a North-South railroad at the foot of the cordillera spurs would open all the Andean valleys; the telegraph is near"

Gerald returned to Lake San Martín in mid-October of 1902, after carrying out reconnaissance tasks under the pitiless conditions of the winter months.

The Limits Treaty signed in London determined that the east coast of Lake San Martín (where the lands of the "Argentine inhabitants" Frank and the Lively brothers were located) was on Argentine soil. The Livelys founded what would later be the *estancia* La Maipú.

When Gerald Lively went to Buenos Aires the Perito Moreno and Colonel Holdich introduced him to President Roca, who thanked him for services rendered. Some time later he traveled to the U.S. for health reasons, leaving his two brothers behind, in Patagonia. When he came back on his last visit, he held several meetings with Francisco P.Moreno. That was one year before his death.

His two brothers, Hugh Robert and Joseph Percy, remained in charge of La Maipú. Eventually, though, the latter decided to return to England and enlisted in the army to fight in the First World War. During that time, owing to a disposition of the Government of Santa Cruz by which all lands that were occupied on a provisional basis had to be legalized by the residents who automatically became rightful owners, Hugh Robert put in his name the near forty thousand hectares he shared with his brother. Nobody ever knew if Hugh had had the intention of putting his brother´s name down and was then faced with legal obstacles to do so in his absence. The fact is that when Joseph Percy returned to Argentina and found out that the title deed was only in Hugh´s name only he got so mad he got close to shooting his brother. There was no way in which Hugh could explain to him that it was just a sheer formality because, in Joseph Percy´s opinion, formality meant something quite different, such as having all the papers in order. Be that as it may, seeing that what should have been in both their names was in Hugh´s name only, he could only conclude that he´d been cheated by his own brother.

That problem marked the end of their relationship. Although they lived at only two kilometers distance, they never set eyes on each other again.

Joseph lived with his wife until she died, in 1957. They had no children. He outlived her for seventeen years and died at the age of 99. In 1942 Hugh Robert sold the *estancia* to don Aureliano Leyenda., He did nothing to make it up to Joseph Percy, financially speaking, he only told the new owner that his brother would continue living on the estate.

Leyenda was an honorable man and never questioned Joseph Percy's presence on his land. Still, as Joseph was proud and not one to take things for granted, he offered to bake bread and cook for them as a show of gratitude for allowing him to stay on at La Maipú. The Leyendas accepted this arrangement, not because they expected retribution but because they realized it was good for Joseph's self-esteem.

During those long years of living in absolute loneliness, Joseph Percy's only communication with the outside world was through an old radio. Nobody ever visited him, neither did he receive any newspapers or magazines. The only package he used to receive by mail was his precious English tea, which Harrod's sent him regularly once a year.

In the house where he led his austere, unassuming existence there is now a museum.

One of the many things Andreas Madsen did when he came to Argentina was to work on the Border Committee under the orders of a fellow countryman, the Danish geographer Ludovico von Platen. He was born in 1881 into a humble peasant family. While still a youngster he became a sailor and came to this part of the world seeking adventure. Drawn by the mystery of Patagonia and mesmerized by the dazzling beauty of the land surrounding the Fitz Roy, he soon realized this was the place he had always dreamed of and where he wanted to stay. He went to Denmark to fetch his fiancée, Fanny, and the newly married couple settled down by the river Las Vueltas, facing the mountain whose beauty never failed to surprise him, in the midst of a landscape he considered a gift of Creation. The Madsens had four children: three boys, and a girl who, when she was still very young chose to live in Buenos Aires, and is the only living member of the family.

Madsen and his friend Fred Ottsen were cornered by the "damned woollies" (the latter's scornful way of addressing the powerful sheep-rearing companies) that expanded at the cost of the small farmers. "They´re arriving with sheep – Fred complained- they´ll be here any minute...If they were a small group of settlers it´s no problem; there´d be rows and fighting but there´d be plenty of space for all of us; but if it´s a company it will gobble everything up".

Madsen, who was only 26 at the time, was sad to see all the settlers next to Lake Viedma resignedly leave their land. He wrote: "I was the only one who stubbornly decided to resist, so I just retreated a few paces, right up to the foot of the Fitz Roy, where I continued fighting, my back to the wall". He believed the real pioneer creates and conquers without predating. On the contrary, destruction is the result of policies applied by the large companies and their unfeeling capital.

Had Madsen had his way national parks would be so vast that the "damned woollies" would automatically be cornered into smaller extensions of land.

Unlike his neighbors, Madsen chose to settle in the beautiful valley facing the Fitz Roy regardless of whether the land was apt for cattle-breeding. For over half a century he enjoyed this "paradise" which he zealously defended breeding animals and planting vegetables and fruit trees. Eventually, that location became a strategic spot for mountain climbers anxious to conquer the Torre or the Fitz Roy. An obliging man, Madsen was always ready to give a hand and was an invaluable support in all expeditions. However, he made it quite clear that he did it "for love of God, not mountain-climbing".

Sometimes he closed his eyes and would let his memory roam to the past and longingly cling to those happy moments when nothing interfered with the placid existence in his paradise. He regretted the disappearance of thousands of deer, gray foxes and other animals which used to follow the rider without fear, and played around the horses´ legs or sat in a circle next to the fire, waiting for a piece of meat or a bone.

Madsen registered all these thoughts in his works. Coincidentally, the scientist Federico Reichert also referred to the amazing tameness of the *huemul* and was outraged by the cruel persecution of these animals which were not to be found in any other part of the world and that would lead to an inevitable extinction. He also remembered those special moments when they were having lunch and the birds were placidly poised on their arms, partaking of the food. It was really like a storybook world. The French author Saint-Loup wrote: "Nothing is written about the Fitz Roy without first mentioning Andréas Madsen at its feet, in his formidable solitude". Madsen left his house to a friend, (another admirer of the Fitz Roy) the German photographer Hern Standhardt. They had met one day when Hern arrived at his place with the idea of taking some pictures. He drove a Ford T which served a multiple purpose as vehicle, laboratory and living quarters. Madsen invited him to stay and they became great friends. When the Danish pioneer retired to Bariloche in the company of his sons, the old photographer was left in charge of the house, where he lived until he died some years later. He left an invaluable legacy of photographs of all the region.

Another of Madsen´s pioneer friends was Alfred Ramstom, from Finland. He lived south of Lake Viedma at the "Helsingfors" *estancia*, which was also used by climbers as a shelter and base.

The Salesian explorer and mountaineer Father De Agostini (who spent his last years in a remote cabin next to the Alps) wrote: "These settlers, as if seized by a mysterious fascination, harbor feelings of deep affection for these solitary Andean valleys".

R. Gorraiz Beloqui was often referred to as "the horseback journalist" because he used to ride long distances gathering notes for his articles. He once said: "In order to see someone in Patagonia one must travel very far. Nobody is ever nearby".

The beautiful Patagonian landscape exerted an enormous power of attraction over travelers and explorers. Nevertheless, its seductive influence was insufficient to attract new inhabitants. Gorraiz Beloqui, who was himself another victim of its charms, regretted not having anybody with whom to share the unique experience of "state of grace" he felt in the furthest and loneliest point of the Patagonian territory. Therefore, he did his best to describe it in his written works.

Once, in 1920, he was descending the cordillera towards the town of Sarmiento, in Chubut. When he got to the location known as Codo de Senguerr he happened to look northwards to see if there was any sign of the river, the outlet of Lake Fontana. What he saw inspired him to write most poetic notes: "What an incredible view! I was amazed, I couldn´t believe my eyes! I had to dismount. The most beautiful, unbelievable mirage covered all that region, which suddenly appeared like a huge city, a truly fantastic, dream-like city. I knew then that it was this vision, or one like it, which originated the legend of the Ciudad de los Césares, with its series of dreams and adventures. That certainty made me feel a state of absolute inner joy".

Still excited by this discovery, Gorraiz Beloqui rode all the way to Sarmiento, unaware of the great distance he covered. He felt the owner of a valuable treasure, that of having found the origin of the most famous legend of Patagonia. He knew then what had lured so many avid fortune seekers to that territory. He suddenly understood the reason why so many expeditions were organized with the sole purpose of finding the mythical city. To go no further, in the expedition led by Hernandarias, there was never any doubt as to the existence of the Ciudad de los Césares; they just thought it was completely out of their reach, so they abandoned the quest without ever realizing they had been seduced by an optical illusion. Apparently, the vision that had kindled such rich fantasies throughout history was produced when the rays of the sun, like the chisel of a sculptor, illuminated the rock formations transforming them into turrets, castles, palaces and other fantastic shapes suggesting a city.

As in ancient Greek literature the call of sirens and nymphs lured the sailors into dangerous waters, so did the magic of Patagonia cast a spell on many travelers who were so anxious to know its secrets that they were willing to run extraordinary risks and even put their life in jeopardy.

According to Gorráiz Beloqui, the magic spell "spurs them on and then makes them stop" indefinitely.

Beloqui once met a public official who asked him point-blank how to get to the mythical city:

> You were there yourself so you can tell me. How does one reach the Ciudad de los Césares?

The "horseback journalist" pointed towards the West and replied:

> Well, it´s as if you wanted to go in that direction and then changed your mind.

13.- THE OUTLAWS

Butch Cassidy, the Sundance Kid and Etta Place were the first famous North American bandits to settle in Patagonia. They installed themselves in Cholila, where they stayed for over four years. Later, other bandits followed suit: there were North Americans, a few Welsh and quite a number of Chileans who were renowned for their cruelty and vicious ways.

Like Cassidy and Sundance Kid, William Wilson and Bob Evans were also North Americans who chose to follow the path of crime. Nevertheless, these two uncouth cowboys did not have the attractive personalities of their predecessors, who had earned the liking of their neighbors and Patagonian friends. Furthermore, they lacked the necessary social graces to mix with the prominent landowners of the district. And as far as cultural background was concerned, they probably never knew what a book looked like.

Butch was quite the opposite. A neighbor once described him as very neat and careful about his appearance, and mentioned certain rituals like putting drops of cologne into the water whenever he washed his hands. And as for culture, this same neighbor pointed out that there were always books to be found in Ryan´s house (Butch was known as Ryan in Argentina).

The bandits in Patagonia were brutal and ruthless. They spread a reign of terror which was a serious threat to settlers. Lest the latter should decide to leave and that the fear of criminals should jeopardize the efforts to attract new inhabitants, the local authorities decided to create a special force to pursue and defeat the outlaws.

The Chief of Police of Comodoro Rivadavia, Horacio Fischer, launched into this pursuit with a crusader´s determination. He was out to get the criminals who had plundered and murdered some settlers of the cordillera. Fischer and his posse rode from the Atlantic coast to Río Mayo and then on to other locations. They traveled over eight hundred kilometers before discovering the hideout of one of the wanted men, José Carrasco. He was a Chilean who had committed eight murders and ten robberies. His gang was made up of the worst kind of criminals who went in for mass killings and indiscriminate slaughter.

Fischer was able to track them down thanks to information given to him by an *Araucano* scout who knew the district backwards and could easily "read" trails.

When the shooting began the criminals, who had obviously been caught unawares, ran out of their hiding place in their underpants. Being unable to see their pursuers who were hiding behind the bushes, Carrasco and his henchmen shot blindly into the air. Knowing who they were up against, Fischer´s men didn´t bother to call a halt, they just shot to kill. Fischer himself decided against calling a cease fire when he saw two of the bandits trying to escape. He would rather have them killed instead of chasing after them on that rocky, uneven terrain. The Indian scout went after them and told the Chief of Police he would leave signs along the way (sticks, crossed twigs, etc.); he knew if he let them go they would inch their way across the cordillera and disappear from view. However, the police managed to catch their prey sooner than they expected: they found them in a stream where Carrasco was cleaning the wounds on his arm. They called a halt. One of the outlaws had a try with his gun and was instantly shot down and killed. Carrasco was turned over to the Chilean police.

Fischer was about to return when he was informed that other criminals were trying to escape by Los Huemules, at the border. These men had bulky police records and their recent crimes had been committed against the terror-stricken inhabitants of the cordillera. Their crime tour included the robbery and murder of Mrs. Elizabeth McEwan in her estancia, continuing with a violent incursion into a store, where they killed the manager (Gregorio Kaminsk) and three other clerks and finally set fire to the premises.

Fischer promised himself and the outraged population to pursue the gang with relentless perseverance. Fury welled up inside him strengthening the bloodthirsty instinct he needed to go after these evil assassins. He went after them day and night, through thickets and over craggy slopes, always seeing in his mind´s eye their evil faces and all their crimes: Francisco Asenjo, who had murdered his brother and, without exception, killed all the victims of his robberies just for kicks. And the three outlaws who had escaped with him: Agustín Elis, Hipólito Reynoso and Francisco Leifill.

Chief Fischer planned a clever ambush and had the outlaws cornered in a location called Laguna Blanca. The shooting lasted several hours. The Indian scout, who was an expert with his lasso, managed to immobilize one of them who was trying to get away. He tied him up and then sat down and waited patiently for the others to appear. Of the two wounded men, one died shortly after and the other managed to survive.

However, Fischer's mission was still not completed. Together with Chilean carabineros they went to Simpson Valley and entered the "Ayson" estancia, taking prisoner another gang of criminals who had robbed and murdered some local colonists.

It took Chief of Police Fischer 17 days to pursue the outlaws, during which time he added an extra 285 leagues to his hazardous itinerary over almost inaccessible trails and mountain passes.

Although his subordinates were considered to be trigger-happy, there was no doubt that crimes and robberies diminished considerably after that bloody event. Maybe it was on that account that the picture of Mr. Foitzich with his wife and nine children in a weekly newspaper didn't pass unnoticed. He was easily recognized as the author of several murders in the outskirts of the border district and was taken prisoner to Puerto Montt. Still, he wasn't a thief, he was just an irascible farmer who had no control over his violent temper. Churlish and hard of speech, his guns became eloquent exponents of his inner rage.

Owing to the large amount of outlaws that ravaged all the western part of Santa Cruz and Chubut, in 1910 the Argentine Government created the Border Police, also known as "The Foreign Legion" on account of the multiple nationalities of its members and the quasi-criminal records of most of them.

That police force distinguished itself in several resounding coups, the most famous of which was probably the capture of the North American gunmen William Wilson and Bob Evans. During a holdup of the Trading Company of Río Pescado, in Chubut, Wilson murdered the manager, the engineer Llwyd Ap Iwan, who was a prominent member of the Welsh community.

Wilson the Texan, not too happy with the income he and Evans got from buying and selling (sometimes even stealing) cattle, was anxious to carry out a hit that would leave them a nice sum of money. Cash of course, which was hard to come by in those parts.

Having found out that a stagecoach carrying the money to pay for the season's wool was on its way to the Trading Company, Wilson and Evans kept their eyes on the road. When they saw the stagecoach approaching they sneaked their way into the premises. They knew the place quite well because it was also a general store where they often bought fishing gear. They went straight up to

Ap Iwan´s office, pointed a gun at him and ordered him to hand over the money that was to pay the sheepshearers. The manager explained that the stagecoach still hadn´t arrived and that there were less than fifty pesos in the safe. They forced him to open the safe anyway. At one moment he hurled himself onto Wilson with the idea of taking the gun from him, but Wilson managed to shoot and the bullet went straight through the manager´s heart.

The scandalous crime infuriated the Welsh settlers who not only had high regard for Ap Iwan because he was a likeable man but also because they respected him for his valuable services as a surveyor, geographer and explorer.

The North American gunmen carried on with their criminal exploits. The Border Police went on a ruthless hunt for them and others of their kind such as Mansel Gibbon, also known as Cameron Jack. He was a son of Daniel Gibbon, a Welshman who had become very friendly with Butch Cassidy and the Sundance Kid when they had their ranch in Cholila.

Eventually, the bandits were overtaken in a hideout in the mountains. During the ensuing crossfire one of the policemen was killed, another was severely wounded, and Wilson and Evans were shot down. On the other hand, Mansel Gibbon managed to escape to Chile.

The Border Police was criticized by most politicians and public officials who frowned upon their unorthodox and "careless" methods. They were also opposed to by congressmen who disapproved of what they considered were "excesses in the repression". In view of these negative opinions, the government dissolved the force in 1918. By that time, many outlaws had been eliminated and criminal activity had begun to decline.

14.- CONQUERING THE INVINCIBLE PEAKS

Inhabitants of the Patagonian Andes were always few and lived very far from one another.

As they grew used to their solitary surroundings they became keen observers and never missed the odd passerby. They occasionally observed newcomers stand in awe in front of the almost sacred beauty surrounding them. Or maybe it was the tenacity of scientists at work, or the enthusiasm of explorers. No matter what the aim was that lured them to this scene, there was always a romantic ideal spurring them on. And that was fine.

However, at some moment they began to resent the presence of suspicious characters prowling around, pretending to be interested in the view. They were wary of these people and their intentions. Their instincts told them these men were not to be trusted.

In spite of their misgivings about visitors´ motivations, and faithful to their proverbial hospitality, the pioneers gave them all the support they requested, which included lodging, food supplies, horses, guides, etc. Somehow, a certain awareness had replaced the former natural welcome given to all newcomers, as if something deep down inside was telling them that from now on things were going to be different. They had become so accustomed to living in solitary freedom that the mere fact of newcomers coming and going was felt as a kind of threat to a way of life they had chosen and that molded their identity.

New characters had appeared on the scene. These were the mountaineers, men whose arrogance the pioneers found distasteful, even insolent. How pretentious of them, to even consider they could succeed in conquering those hitherto impregnable peaks!

They regarded these visitors with ambivalence. In the first place, because they themselves knew all about putting up with hardships and taking risks, and so they admired these men for their spirit and courage. On the other hand, they resented them for being so presumptuous, so ready to assault the unapproachable beauty of their sanctuary.

Eventually, they had to admit these intruders had many of the qualities of the pioneers: the motivation of a powerful goal which they pursued tenaciously and the skill to guarantee success in their undertakings.

It was with mixed feelings that they observed mountaineers climbing those impossible heights inch by inch, clinging on to minute pieces of rock the size of a thumbnail, crawling up vertical stone walls, risking their lives every minute in their overpowering desire to reach the summit.

The history of mountain climbing in the Andes is divided into two different periods, the first of which we could call romantic, and a latter stage which is characterized by a display of technical resources and a high level of proficiency. The Torre and the Fitz Roy are the most challenging mountains in the world. The conquest of these peaks of the Hielo Patagónico is the highest mark a climber can aspire to. However, during the past century it was the Aconcagua that occupied a privileged position in the history of mountaineering, featuring dramatic episodes, some of which show the dangers faced by daring climbers, others that tell poignant, touching stories of people who met a tragic death on one of its slopes.

The first attempt to conquer an Andean peak was in 1883, when the German scientist Paul Güssfeldt ventured on the 7000-meter-high Aconcagua. He managed to reach the 6200 mts. mark. Another endeavor was carried out in 1897 by an Englishman, Edward Fitz Gerald, and his expedition. Three of its members –Matías Zürbriggen in the first place, later followed by Stuart Vines and Nicolás Lanti- reached the summit. They left Vines´s ice axe and a thermometer as evidence of their feat. In 1906 the researchers Federico Reichert and Roberto Helbling climbed the Aconcagua. Only the latter was able to reach the summit, and the trophy he brought down was none other than Vines´s ice axe.

Although there were many climbing expeditions after that, it was only in 1925 that the summit was reached once again. On that opportunity it was M.F. Rojan, C.W. Macdonald and J. Cochrane who made it, bringing down with them the thermometer that had been left by Vines together with a card: "M.W.S. Vines, Fikerton Rectory Lincoln".

During a very cold winter in 1928, the English explorer Basil Marden left a very ambiguous letter in the Puente del Inca Hotel. The contents of the note, which were made public by Federico Reichert, were the following: "If I were to die, this statement absolves the residents of Puente del Inca of all responsibility. I have set no date for my return. I don´t need any search parties looking for me".

The enigmatic explorer never returned. A few months later Marden´s dead body was found on a part of the mountain slope called Los Horcones. He was buried in Puente del Inca. Opinions were divided between those who believed him to be mentally unbalanced and those who thought he had committed suicide.

That same year there was another fatal accident, that of the Austrian mountain climber José Stipanich. His body, which was found by Hans George Link at 6.800 m, was in a position that suggested he had been resting or asleep at the time of his death. He had frozen in a seated position on a stone, and the snow covered his body like a shroud.

Since then, many expeditions came from all over the world to climb America´s highest peak, some of them resulting in formidable feats and others in equally dramatic failure. Without exception, they all endured almost inhuman weather conditions. White wind, violent snowstorms, freezing cold, were a permanent threat to andinists.

In 1934 two expeditions reached the summit along different routes. One was Italian, the "Crociera alle Ande", which included an Argentine member, Lieutenant Nicolás Plantamura. The other was Polish and included the alpine climbers Narkievicz, Dañzycki, Ostrowski, Karpinski and Osiecki. These carried out a remarkable prowess climbing the difficult East-Northeast slope, which was named Glaciar de los Polacos in their honor.

In March of 1936 Hans George Link climbed the Aconcagua alone, in absolute solitude. After that he was known as the "solitary condor". He was excited as well as moved by the discovery of the photograph of a young, beautiful woman, with the following inscription written on its back:

"Solo il sogno e musica, e la realta caduca materia que si corrompe e muta. (In memoria de la nostra giovinezza). Cordialmente, Pina".

And the request that whoever should happen to find the picture to please forward it to Dott. Pina Ungaro – Milano (Via P. Coletta 10). On December 25th 1936, Hans George Link personally delivered the picture to its owner.

The Alpine Climbers Club of Mendoza organized an important expedition for the months of February and March of 1936, under the technical leadership of Hans George Link, accompanied by his wife, Adrienne Bance. Doctor Eduardo Carette, President of the Argentine Scientific Society, was in charge of the scientific direction. Other members were Dr. Walter Schiller, Deputy Director of the La Plata Museum, a qualified team of botanists, geographers, meteorologists and university professors, as well as communications staff, a cameraman and a group of mountaineers. In all there were twenty-two men and ten women. Among the latter was Professor A. Palese de Torres, whose travel diary, later published by Ediciones Geográficas Argentinas, proved to be a valuable record of the expedition.

The team set off on their journey motivated by a shared excitement. The sole idea of climbing the Aconcagua sent a thrill through these men and women who felt they were on the verge of important discoveries and hitherto unknown sensations. Professor Palese´s diary begins like this: "Aconcagua! This mountain, so rich in fantasies and traditions, can fulfill the highest aspirations of daring mountaineers and eager geologists. (...) At sundown, when the last rays of sun paint the peak in hues of red, the summit of the Aconcagua seems to be on fire, like some sort of fantastic volcano".

The organizing committee gave all members of the expedition literature that covered the different circumstances they might have to go through. Therefore, they were appropriately warned about the treacherous charms of the mountain, and they were given sound advice regarding several practical matters, such as how to prevent mountain sickness, how to counteract the excessive dryness of the mountain air or when to proceed with self-examination to be on guard against shock. Due attention should be given to fatigue and drowsiness, both of which are valuable guidelines for determining the extent of physical resistance.

It was time to leave. The muleteer was getting the mules ready. Every now and then he took a grim look at the thick, steel-gray clouds that covered the sky and seemed to announce a snowstorm. As if seized by a sense of foreboding, he shook his head and said: "I hope I´ll get to see you all again".

"A shiver ran through us –wrote A. Palese de Torres- when we suddenly remembered all those who rest on the slope of the Aconcagua under the immaculate shroud of snow: Captain Marden, Stepanich and, more recently, the Chileans Solari and Ruperto".

However, the grim feeling disappeared as soon as they saw H. G.Link approaching, riding his mule and playing sweet Tyrolean tunes on his harmonica. He had a natural gift for making everybody feel safe and secure in his presence.

Those who had no previous experience in mountaineering went through a rough time during the climb. They still weren´t accustomed to the bad weather and the freezing cold which they found, at times, unbearable. Although the women slept fully dressed, they never managed to get warm. According to the diary, the gusts of wind were increasingly violent and even blew into the tent. "Piolín", a dog that belonged to one of the muleteers had become very popular among the members of the group, helping them to keep their feet warm. Still, maybe it tired of its new role and, to everyone´s distress, it returned to Puente del Inca. "Nobody was able to sleep. We were worried lest the wind blasts should blow our tent away. Outside, the mules could be heard moaning on account of the freezing cold. Apparently, the temperature was many degrees below zero. The hours went by and still nobody was able to sleep. At eleven a.m. the wind calmed down and we managed to go out of our tent. Then the group started to split up, when two of the members decided to go back. We were suddenly seized by a feeling of apprehension. That afternoon two mountaineers descended from the 6200 meter camp bringing with them Fifi, the Links´ dog. They were still terrified from their experience with the "white wind". They seemed very sick and complained about the dreadful headaches brought about by the intense cold. They´d lost a lot of weight and looked deathly pale. In spite of their pitiable physical condition their eyes shone when they described the beautiful scene that surrounded them. They were under the magic spell of the Andes. They said the higher you get the more magnificent the view. The atmosphere becomes transparent and it is even possible to see the Pacific Ocean on the other side of the Chilean mountain range. Peaks multiply in an unending array.

Link returned shortly after. He had gone to rescue a member of the group and looked exhausted after 28 hours of uninterrupted climbing up the ice-covered slope. He said that although they were desperately in need of sleep they would take turns: one kept watch while the other slept for ten minutes. Only ten minutes. One must never forget that death is constantly lurking in the violent ice-cold gusts of wind.

The High Mountain Committee carried out research tasks in the Cuerno and Güssfeldt Glaciers, based on studies by Güssfeldt himself, Fitz Gerald and Federico Reichert, who was at the time considered the topmost authority in the matter.

The mountain was estimated as having different heights: in 1887, Güssfeldt, 6,970 meters. 1897, Fitz Gerald, 7,035; Chilean border committee, 6,960; Argentine border committee, 7,130; in 1904, Schrader, 6,953; in 1940, Link, 7,036 and the estimate of the Reichert-Helbling expedition was 7,010 meters average with an approximate error of 32 meters.

15.- CELEBRATION OF MASS ON THE MOUNTAIN

On the morning of a very cold day, the arrival of a stranger interrupted the daily routine at the camp. The women hastily finished drinking their hot toddy and went out of the tent to have a look. To their surprise, they came face to face with a priest, Father José Kastelic, who was traveling to Chile and had made a halt in order to say Sunday Mass.

He was a 42-year-old Yugoslav who had been ordained in Ljubijana. He was traveling to Chile on a priestly mission and had come all the way from Buenos Aires, where he used to celebrate daily Mass at 10 a.m. in the San José de Flores Basilica. On the way he stopped to get a bearing of his surroundings. He was spellbound by the magnificent view of the cordillera seen from Puente del Inca. After saying Mass in Plaza de Mulas and, due to the sudden illness of the expedition´s priest, Father Kastelic decided to take his place and accompany the group himself.

The following morning he began to feel the first symptoms of mountain sickness and requested permission to lie down. He was contemplating the possibility of returning to Plaza de Mulas when a certain rumor made him change his mind. According to information gathered by some of the members of the expedition, it was considered possible to recover the body of José Stepanich, who had died 14 years before. Therefore, the priest decided to stay in order to bless the remains of the mountaineer.

In the meantime, several members of the group were forced to return, some to Mendoza, others to La Plata and Buenos Aires, to resume their studies or for professional reasons.

The only remaining members were the Links, Father Kastelic and ten others, six of which were due to leave in just a few days.

According to the customary medical examinations, all members of the expedition were in fit condition to reach the final goal, which was to reach the summit. Owing to Father Kastelic´s later inclusion in the group, he hadn´t undergone the clinical checkup. Furthermore, the instrument for measuring blood pressure had gone out of order on account of the cold. Out of caution, the physician of the expedition, Doctor Roque Polito, advised the priest not to climb beyond 5.000 meters. Eventually they set off, and the priest said he felt very well. When they reached a particularly dangerous spot, Link advised him not to advance any further. There were big blocks of ice that could easily give way. If anything happened to him nobody would see him because visibility was reduced to two meters at most, and if he called out nobody would hear him on account of the deafening noise of the wind beating on the rocks. The priest said they were not to worry about him and went on his way. Still, after advancing only a few paces he sat down on a rock. He made the sign of the Cross and started to pray out loud both in Latin and in Yugoslav. The others resumed their climb. Their last glimpses of the priest showed him resting and holding his head between his hands. Finally, the group made it to the summit. On their return, they saw Father Kastelic in the same position they had left him in. On seeing them, he remarked:

"When you were up there, I found the ice-axe that belonged to the Chileans (two unfortunate mountaineers who died during an attempt to reach the summit). This is it".

"Father –answered Link- do you remember what your ice-axe looked like? Do you remember it had a protruding rivet that was twisted? This ice-axe does not belong to the Chileans, it´s yours".

The priest immediately started to talk about God´s kindness. He picked up a stone and said:

"Do you think this stone would be here if God hadn´t willed it?"

Of course everybody readily agreed and then tried to persuade him to join them in the descent.

"It´s getting late, Father, and we must descend before nightfall".

The members of the expedition were exhausted. After arduous climbing with very bad weather and having to face situations where their lives ran serious risks, the mere act of speaking was a strenuous effort. Nevertheless, the priest was adamant. He refused to stand up and expressed his firm determination to stay. He told Link he was willing to write a note saying he had decided to stay of his own free will, thus freeing him from all responsibility. He was so firm in his decision that they finally let him have his own way. In any case, they weren´t going far. Just 150 meters until they reached the camp at 6.700 meters where they planned to spend the night. They even planned on taking turns to visit him until they could convince him to go back with them. They secured his tent, checked the heater, the food supply and his sleeping bag. When they were sure everything was in order, they left. Next morning they approached his tent but he was nowhere to be seen. They presumed he must have attempted to climb. The Links went back later that same day but he still wasn´t there. In vain they looked around for him and finally gave him up for lost.

His body was found one year later by the expedition led by Lieutenant Emiliano Huerta, at 5.700 meters height. Just by chance they tried to remove a piece of white cloth lying on the snow and discovered underneath it a tent covering a body.

They carried him down by mule and buried him next to the chapel in Puente del Inca.

16.- THE PREMONITION

The first member of the expedition to reach the summit was Pablo Franke and the rest then followed suit. Among them was Adrienne Bance de Link, who was the first woman to accomplish the feat.

They embraced and cried together, sharing that special moment on top of the world.

They stayed for a lapse of four hours during which they made a survey of the summit following Link´s instructions. He calculated the surface to be around 40 by 60 meters. On the south side there was a 3000 meters´ deep precipice, the bottom of which was concealed by thick clouds. They were quite surprised to see that there was neither snow nor ice accumulated on the top of the mountain. It didn´t take them long to realize that the violent wind beating on the rock was what prevented the snow from depositing.

At one moment Link apologized to them for having been very nervous, and explained that irritability and bad temper were a direct consequence of the decrease of atmospheric pressure. Everybody claimed having felt the same, cold, exhausted and feeling that they were at the end of their tether.

All the women had tremendous admiration for Adrienne Link, and in a way they secretly resented her husband for having submitted her to such a strenuous ordeal. She seemed so small and fragile, nobody could fathom where she found the strength to persevere in the achievement of such a challenging goal. Not only was she delicate and gracious, she was also very straightforward and everybody respected her for it. She was convinced, and said so outwardly, that her recklessness could cost her her life. There seemed to be no end to her fatigue and need of sleep and yet she continued on, following her husband almost automatically, in silence, with not a word of complaint.

She was awarded the Golden Condor as a prize for her prowess, which was flattering of course, although the fact of receiving the trophy also made her aware of what could have been her fate if she had surrendered to the "white wind". She knew then that her tenacious resistance had saved her from one of the main enemies in mountaineering: sleep. An unwritten law of the mountain says one must never give in to the sweet temptation of sleep because it dulls the senses and numbs consciousness, leading to a frozen rest from which one will never awake.

In her diary, Professor A. Palese de Torres described Adrienne Link´s nervous condition: "Depression became evident in the fatigue that took possession of her fragile self. Every object became heavy in her mind. Her legs frequently gave way; the lethal sleep was always there, threatening to defeat her; there was a dull look in her eyes, as if she was secretly crying, and a deathly anguish wrung her heart. Adrienne was stubbornly determined to reach the top because that´s what he wanted her to do".

No matter what the situation, Hans Link himself used to stretch his physical resistance to the limit. Whenever he returned from his solitary ascents or from a rescue party where he had once again demanded the utmost effort from his disciplined self, it was always Adrienne who surrounded him with comforting care until he recovered completely.

Once he returned worn out after another fruitless search for Father Kastelic and was forced to go out immediately to the rescue of the geologist Walter Schiller and another member of the expedition who, due to a raging storm were stranded in the 6.400 mt. camp. He found both men in a fearful state, with Schiller even beginning to show symptoms of a nervous breakdown. They were carried down to Plaza de Mulas.

The following morning Link decided to go off on another search for Father Kastelic. Although it was unwise of him to leave without at least that day´s rest, nobody had the courage to tell him so. In a way, all those acquainted with him knew it was his way of doing things; self-sacrifice on behalf of goals he had set himself always drove him to the very limit of his endurance.

In February of 1944, during the preliminaries for another expedition on the Aconcagua, the writer Tibor Sekelj was visiting the Links at their home.

He was quite intrigued by Adrienne whom he described as being rather like a toy: petite and well proportioned, always smiling and with her fair curls perfectly neat and orderly.

Those who met her found it hard to believe that this fragile, delicate person was the same self-willed woman who had performed the remarkable feat of climbing the highest peak in America. Confusion increased on hearing her soft voice with a marked French accent, definitely more conceivable in the undertones of a dainty "salon" than carried away by the raging wind at seven thousand meters´ height.

Link loved to greet mountaineers in his home, he therefore invited Tibor Sekelj to talk about his favorite subject.

On this occasion, and following a ritual he performed with all his guests, he inquired:

"Have you seen Aconcagua mushrooms?"

As was to be expected, everybody said no. He would then address his wife:

"Mon petit chou, would you please bring the mushrooms?"

And she would appear holding a jar which she promptly placed in the guest´s hands. It definitely didn´t look like mushrooms, and the visitor would generally turn the jar over in his hands with a perplexed look on his face while he observed the strange looking objects. Only after making sure that suspense clung heavily did Link oblige with an explanation:

"These are no mushrooms. These are the eight toes that were cut off when my feet froze during the 1942 expedition. Just because one night I slept with my shoes on. I felt nothing at first, then I was unable to walk and the toes went blue. It was gangrene and something had to be done, and quick".

"That was when I took the scissors and cut the toes off "–said Adrienne-.

They had a long chat during which Link always spoke of the mountain with a worshipper´s respect; he even confided to his guest that the Aconcagua was the only peak he considered worth climbing.

Among the members of the ensuing expedition were Sekelj, Mario Bertone, the 65-year-old naturalist and geologist Walter Schiller and Alberto Kneidt, a young engineer who was eager to attempt his first climb up the Aconcagua, - among other reasons because, in strict keeping with a high-mountain diet, he could eat onions and garlic to his heart´s content without having to worry about his breath. Last but not least was Fifi, the Link´s little dog that had reached the summit for the first time in 1940.

The cold they suffered during the climb was extreme even by Aconcagua standards. Gusts of wind slapped their clothes and filled their mouths and eyes with snow. It was the fearful "white wind", frequently present at great heights but a rare visitor in Plaza de Mulas. All the beer bottles had frozen and exploded, and they had to dig under the snow to rescue the odd tin or food container.

The expedition split into groups. While some of the members were unable to leave the shelter on account of the storm, others continued to the 6.200 meters level. There Schiller set up camp and two of the members decided to return. They had all lost contact with Link and young Kneidt, who were supposedly advancing towards the summit.

Lack of news of the other groups obviously worried those who had remained behind in the shelter. Still, they were comforted by the thought that they must surely have sought protection at the 6.200 meters level until the end of the windstorm. When eventually the storm did calm down they set off on a search for the Links, Schiller and Kneidt. They reached the 6500 meters and there was still no trace of them. They shouted their names and received no answer but the echo of their own voices.

They hopefully left some food and supplies in the shelter –later named after Link- and in Nido de Cóndores. A feeling of dark pessimism got hold of them after three days of not hearing from their companions. They finally decided to return to base. During the descent they anxiously looked around them just in case, but deep down in their hearts they suspected the worst had already happened.

They conjectured about Schiller´s death and the reasons he might have had for refusing to descend from the 6.200 meters. All these doubts were reinforced when they found him frozen outside the sleeping bag. Although he appeared to be physically fit he did show signs of certain mental disturbance which was apparently a consequence of the 1914 war.

Putting two and two together they reached the following conclusions: before the climb he had repeatedly stated that if he were to die he would rather it happened on the Aconcagua. Had he gone there to die? On six different opportunities over the last forty years he had unsuccessfully tried to reach the top. On this occasion he had reached the highest level at 6.200 meters. As usual when a frozen body is found, the lips were set in a sort of fixed smile. Somebody suggested it was a smile of happiness for having fulfilled a deep, secret desire.

Once the disappearance of the Links was confirmed a search committee led by Emiliano Huerta was sent to rescue the remains of the climbers. It was a long, disheartening search, with all the drawbacks and none of the thrilling excitement typical of any ascent. In order to carry out a thorough search they were forced to make many detours which was very tiring and on many occasions they were tempted to give up. Suddenly, at approximately one hundred and fifty meters from the top, a voice resounded:

"I found a body!"

It was Hans George Link´s body, lying horizontally, with his head leaning on a rock and the feet in a resting position. One year had elapsed since death caught up with him when he was resting. And since then nothing had changed.

At about fifty meters´ distance somebody discovered a bulky shape. It was Adrienne Link´s body, which was twisted into a forced position, her head thrown back on a crevice. Under the balaclava there was a frozen expression of pain and her face was burnt by the cold and the icy wind. Beside her were her husband´s ice axe and goggles, which was most puzzling because no climber ever parts with these items. Adrienne´s ice axe was found three meters away. The little dog, Fifi, was never found.

The mountaineers tried to figure out the possible sequence of events that led to these tragic deaths. They assumed that during the descent, -and probably due to the violent wind and snowstorm- Adrienne Link must have had a fall that caused a serious fracture. Her husband went to her aid, and when he realized it was already too late he tenderly covered her face with her balaclava. Such was his state of shock and bereavement that when heading for camp he forgot his ice axe and goggles, both indispensable items during a storm. After fifty meters he stopped to rest. Apart from physical exhaustion, he felt depressed and downhearted. He must have rested too long for he never woke up from the heavy sleep in arms of the lethal white wind.

Kneidt´s body was found a year later, about a hundred meters down.

The Links were buried in the cemetery of Puente del Inca, and Professor Schiller in La Plata. Their fellow climbers would have liked a different resting place for their colleagues. They would much rather have buried the Links near the summit of the Aconcagua and Walter Schiller at the 6.200 level.

News of the Links´ tragic death rapidly got around. For months army aircraft had flown over the area where they had disappeared. During all that time, there was the secret hope that maybe they had survived after all. So when they finally found the bodies the news came like an anticlimax. Suspense sadly drew to an end.

In the same way as tragic love stories became famous on the movie screen, this couple became a symbol of romantic *"andinism"*.

17.- "ANDINISM": LEGENDS AND TECHNIQUE

In Quichua, Aconcagua means "Sentry of Stone". This name hardly expresses all the power and magnetism of its majestic stature nor the thick fabric of legend and prowess woven through decades of intrepid mountaineering. Almost one hundred eager climbers lost their lives trying to conquer its challenging walls.

Climbing the normal –or classical- route didn´t require major technical skills. On the other hand, the south slope did demand technical prowess and was therefore a coveted goal for expert mountain climbers who were not prepared to waste their time and effort on mediocre climbing projects. Landmarks in the history of technical climbing were the French team and the Polish ascent in 1934.

The history of the Aconcagua is not only about mountaineering. Expeditions have also brought to light important discoveries, such as an Inca cemetery at 5300 meters´ height, enclosed between two huge dry-stone walls in an out-of-the-way location seldom frequented by climbers. In 1985 a team of the *Andinists* Club of Mendoza discovered what would later be called "The Mummy of the Aconcagua". The rescue expedition that was subsequently organized included three of the climbers who had discovered it, as well as archaeologists and ethnologists. The funerary bundle that wrapped the "mummy" was preserved within a one-meter-diameter circle of stones on permafrost ground and placed next to a niche containing six golden statuettes. The "mummy" was the body of a seven or eight-year-old boy which had been anointed with red paint and swathed in numerous layers of cloth. According to experts, it was offered to the Gods as a sacrifice, presumably because they had gained control over new territory, or because the Inca had died. For these occasions, a pure and immaculate being was chosen to be God´s messenger; this was considered a great honor. Besides the sun, the Incas also adored the high mountains which they believed to be the source of life, strength and fertility.

Basically, there are three main routes to climb the Aconcagua: the standard route, which is the best known; no technical expertise is required, and bad weather is the major enemy *andinists* must contend with. Then there is the

Glaciar de los Polacos, definitely a more challenging goal, and finally the South wall, which is only apt for expert climbers who have mastered the most sophisticated technical skills.

The South wall is a huge, intimidating ice block which always looks on the verge of collapsing and crushing all those who wish to conquer it. It is one of world´s largest walls and among the most difficult to climb. According to Lionel Terray, a living legend of French mountaineering (he had also recently attacked the Fitz Roy), it posed a colossal problem for climbers. His words may have been meant to daunt his colleagues, in which case they produced precisely the opposite effect. In fact, very soon all his fellow climbers were gathering around the Aconcagua and planning their next onslaught. Among them were six famous names, real champions in those days: G.Poulet, R. Paragot, P. Lesseur, L. Berardini, A. Dagory and E. Denis. It took them one month to get over the preliminaries and to become acclimatized, and one whole strenuous week to reach the summit. Everything was against them. The rocks were unstable, the ice forced them to take extra precautions, the weather couldn´t have been colder. All the more credit to them, who left their imprint on one of the toughest accesses on a world scale.

At the time, the feat carried out by the French was qualified as "heroic bravado". Nevertheless, it was the first of a series and in 1966 there were at least three other ascents: an Argentine expedition, an Austrian-Argentine and also a Japanese team.

Many are the factors that make this new route so dangerous: one of them is the quality of the rock, which is unstable and therefore in constant danger of crumbling or starting an avalanche. Then there is the unevenness of a slope which is also at enormous height above sea level. And the abrupt changes of merciless weather. Not to mention the eerie sensations produced by overwhelming isolation.

Some ascents had a tragic end, like the American expedition, where two of the climbers met their death after having reached the top. The ice axe they had left on the summit was brought down by a team of qualified Argentine *andinists*: Guillermo Vieiro, Pipo Frasson and Fermín Olaechea on the first rope, and Héctor Cuiñas, Eliseo Busto and Jorge Vitón in the second.

Before the ascent of the South wall in 1973, they made a conscientious assessment of the different routes. When faced with such a challenging situation, choosing the correct route is a basic rule. The climb was extremely dangerous and demanded maximum effort on the part of all those concerned. Fortunately, after a first rough period the weather became quite mild. There was an unusual, comforting calm in the clear sky that sundown was dyeing with hues of pink.

Suddenly, there was a tremor down below and the whole mountain seemed to shake. A gust of white-powder wind whirled near the climbers, who were caught in the middle of what seemed like an earthquake, and then they heard a thunderous noise. Like a stroke of lightning, an ice avalanche zigzagged furiously down the slope and the mountain appeared to crack.. A destructive force arising from its very heart disrupted its white magnificence and tons of ice crumbled into the valley while powdery clouds danced madly at the foot of the slope.

The mountaineers looked on, stunned by the deafening sound and mesmerized by the white cataclysm that seemed to be a prelude of the end.

Then, in what seemed a miraculous turn of fortune, they saw that there was still no sign of an avalanche on the route they had chosen.

That night they hardly slept. Partly on account of the cold (25° below zero), but also because they knew that, beyond any reasonable doubt, the next morning they might reach the summit.

Putting all technical drawbacks behind them, they hopefully set out on what they expected would be the last trek. They trudged through the snow with painstaking slowness. The summit was so near and yet so far! At times they thought they´d never make it, specially when they were stuck knee-deep in the snow and felt so tired they feared they wouldn´t be able to move their legs. They went beyond the 6.900 meters and suddenly, there it was: the summit, just a kilometer away from where they stood.

Although the wind lashed at them mercilessly, these men covered those few, never-ending meters driven by the obsession of reaching the top. As they were professional mountaineers, they were aware that the ritual of planting the flag and the ice-pick was only a part of the prowess and that full victory came only upon returning safe and sound to base. But they also knew that nothing could equal the emotion of that magic moment when they reached the top of the highest peak of America.

They stood there, speechless and imbued by an awesome, sacred feeling that comes in that fleeting instant when they become one with the wind, the sky and the mountain.

In view of that extremely intense sensation one is inclined to doubt the words of many mountaineers when they say that nature in such a grandiose scale makes them feel small and insignificant. Quite the contrary, deep down inside they must know they have accomplished a major achievement, a trophy they never would have conquered had they not pledged all their faith and willpower. Even if it cost them their life.

18.- ICE CATHEDRALS

The wind, nature´s patient artist, took millions of years to sculpt the fantastic stone cathedrals of the Hielos Continentales. Its chisel tamed the rock with violent strokes, creating weird, extraordinary shapes with the vehemence typical of its style. The Torre and Fitz Roy are its masterpieces in the region of Hielos Patagónicos. These two peaks are almost inaccessible. They are coveted by the world´s most outstanding mountaineers who must always aim higher in order to maintain international prestige. And because after all, what can be compared to the wonder of looking at the world from the top of the Cerro Torre!

It is often said that whoever is lucky enough to climb the Fitz Roy and the Cerro Torre on a clear day will be able to see a vast horizon of icy peaks on the Eastern slope of the Southern Hielo Patagónico that most climbers don´t even know exist.

Hielo Patagónico is situated in the heart of the cordillera, covering the area from the San Valentín mountain up North to Lago Argentino down South, some 430 km. in length. In width, it can vary between 80 km. in the northern sector and 30 km. in the south.

Although most of it is on Chilean territory, the peaks most coveted by mountain climbers are in the Argentine province of Santa Cruz.

Nobody lives in the Hielo Patagónico. Nevertheless, every now and then it is penetrated by daring people who wish to explore its mysteries or feel the thrill of a major challenge. The passion that urges them on must be very powerful in order to face the constant storms, hurricane winds and damp, heavy clouds that cover those desolate, icy plains.

The first attempt to venture into the Hielo Patagónico was in 1914, by an expedition in charge of the naturalist Federico Reichert. The team groped its way across thirty endless kilometers until they reached a narrow pass where they established the main dividing line of the waters. That pass was later named after Reichert.

Later incursions carried out by Father Alberto María De Agostini and Reichert himself yielded important discoveries. In a way, they were pioneers in exploring these icy regions and became a symbol of the romantic Andean period. Since then there have been many expeditions led by explorers of worldwide fame who were lured by the enigmatic, desolate Hielos Patagónicos.

The Fitz Roy is the highest mountain peak in that region and was the first to excite the ambition of famed mountaineers eager to dare its imposing height – 3441 m- It owes its name to the "Perito" Moreno, although the Indians called it Chaltén (volcano). Like the Torre (3128 m), it is formed by volcanic rocks and surrounded by needles and peaks which have developed over a period of some twelve million years.

In 1937, a team of Italian mountaineers organized by the famous explorer Count Aldo Bonacossa attempted an assault on the Fitz Roy. Andreas Madsen was a silent and disapproving witness of all the preliminaries. He believed it was a useless and even sacrilegious action. That implacable mountain would undoubtedly bury all manifestations of human vanity. However, in this as in other expeditions, he offered his generous collaboration. In fact, his estancia became the base for all the expeditions that arrived to climb the different peaks of the region.

Bonacossa´s attempt, together with others in 1947 and 1948, ended in failure, all of which seemed to prove that Madsen´s idea was correct: that magnificent stone cathedral was there to teach vain and bragging men a lesson.

It was only in 1952 that a Frenchman, Lionel Terray, together with young Guido Magnone, managed to reach the summit. The organizer of the expedition was M.A. Azema. He wrote a book about the Fitz Roy and the legend that had been woven around it: the mountain that Madsen believed had been created by God to show the futility of human pride.

Madsen was shattered; he never overcame the shock of seeing his beliefs torn to bits. Eventually he left the district. Many pragmatists considered his ideas were just some kind of superstition. Still, he had managed to put the fear of God into some of the Frenchmen, who were impressed by his ominous warnings. In a way, they believed in some kind of tragic premonition, and all future events that ended in tragedy seemed to confirm this somber theory. When Henri Poincenot, a member of the team, drowned trying to wade through the choppy waters of the river Las Vueltas, it was readily assumed that his death had occurred because of some sort of divine revenge. Although there was also another version, and that was that he had seduced a beautiful estanciera and her jealous husband killed him out of spite.

The climb had been very difficult. Whenever there were signs of an approaching storm, Terray thought of abandoning the challenge. According to Azema, they continued thanks to the insistence of Magnone, who was determined to reach the summit "...even at the cost of his life".

"If we manage to get the pitons in, it's done: the Fitz Roy is ours!"

His luck depended on a piton. Magnone looked at his belt and saw he only had two pitons left, both crooked and in pretty bad shape. He took one of them out of his belt, placed it with great care and gave a soft stroke with the hammer: the piton broke and fell. He then tried his luck with the second and last piton: using the hammer he managed to get it half a centimeter into the rock but the edges crumbled and the piton didn't stay in place. In these situations one needs an "ace of hearts, a small piton with a very fine blade". And –continues Azema- "Magnone weeps with rage and despair: We've lost, Lionel, we've lost"

Terray stared into empty space, as if trying to remember something. Yes, in fact, he remembered having used an "ace of hearts" to open a tin of sardines at the camp... and, hadn't he put it away in his knapsack? If so, it must be there. He started rummaging in his bag. Magnone was practically having a fit. Suddenly, there it was! A triumphant Lionel Terray produces his trophy and both men laugh and shout for joy.

From there it was straight up to the top. The men embraced and looked at the fascinating white world that opened before them.

Lionel Terray afterwards wrote a book, "Les conquérants de l'inutile", where he described that feat. In his opinion, comparing the Fitz Roy with all the other ascents he had accomplished, "it was the climb that demanded the most of my physical and psychical energies. Technically speaking, it might be considered inferior to the climbs on the granite walls of the Alps. However, a great climb takes much more than the sum of its lengths of rope".

The next attempt was carried out by the Argentines José Luis Fonrouge and Carlos Comesaña, who reached the summit using the route of the Supercanaleta. Their style of climbing was surprisingly modern and audacious, because they didn't use ropes. It took them three days to go up and down, in January of 1965.

Although many latter expeditions reached the top, success was never easy. In 1969 a group from California called "The Fun Hogs" tried their luck. A violent storm caught them on the way up, forcing them to dig holes in the snow to seek shelter in. Their blockade lasted six days, after which they climbed for thirty hours to reach the summit. They followed what is even now considered the most beautiful and classic route.

1976: the Italian team "Arañas de Lecco" ("Spiders of Lecco"), under the leadership of Casimiro Ferrari, brought with them highly sophisticated gear. They even had a cable car specially designed to transport equipment. Ferrari wrote: "We were on the IIIrd degree and up to that moment the going was easy. Suddenly I lost my balance and was sent flying towards Meles. My face hit against the rock and I stood still, suspended by the rope. I felt something hot in my mouth. It was blood. I'd lost some teeth. I thought to myself "if I give up and go down, tomorrow I might not be able to climb again". So we continued on. When we were only thirty meters away from the top a thick fog closed upon us. Afraid that it would make us lose our sense of direction we built a bivouac, and waited. Eventually the sun came out. First Vittorio Meles and then myself, we both touched the summit, in the glorious sunlight".

January of 1979: A remarkable achievement was that of Renato Casarotto, from Vicenza, who ventured on his own and was the first to climb up the north pillar of the Fitz Roy. Another solitary mountaineer was a Frenchman, Ives Astier who, in 1985 reached the summit after only twelve hours´ climb, following the route formerly traced by the Californian group. His record was surpassed the following year by an Austrian, the lone climber Thomas Bubendorfer, who reached the summit in only seven and a half hours.

There were also women in some of the successful expeditions.

The Patagonian range with its magnificent peaks and dazzling white glaciers has a magnetism that seems to attract mountain climbers and explorers from all over the world, who are willing to risk their lives for a taste of freedom in its absolute expression.

Quoting the words of the mountain climber Giuliano Maresi, there "one feels nature breathing".

19.- THE TORRE: THE MOST DIFFICULT PEAK

Climbing the Torre is like fighting a duel with a fearless and extremely skillful rival. Only very expert mountaineers can attempt the challenge. This fine, piercing silhouette topped by an ice cap has inspired a rich and original saga.

Andinists who are very meticulous about dates and historical facts have reason to believe that the first to climb the Torre was the Italian Casimiro Ferrari. Yet it is another Italian, Cesari Maestri, who claims to have been the first to reach the top. There is no actual proof of his ascent because the person who was in charge of taking the photographs -the Austrian Toni Egger- fell off the mountain and his body was never recovered. Many climbers are inclined to doubt Maestri´s word.

At first, nobody thought it was possible to climb this forbidding stone needle. F.Azema wrote: "even thinking of it is vain and ridiculous". Héctor Castiglioni - a well-known mountaineer who took part in the first attempt to climb the Fitz Roy with Count Bonacossa- said that climbing the Torre seemed impossible "even to those who, like me, always think of mountains and peaks in terms of hypothetical accessibility".

Nevertheless, far from discouraging prospective climbers, all these comments seemed to lure them on. In Father De Agostini´s opinion, the overpowering vertical walls carved on the glacier were a tempting challenge for international champions always intent on improving their records.

Many of those who decided to ignore nature´s final limits paid for their recklessness with their lives. Deep down inside they are transgressors.

The first attempt to climb the Torre was in 1957. Due to bad weather conditions and other technical problems the head of the expedition, Bruno Detassis, gave the order to turn back. He was an experienced climber who considered the Torre was an "impossible mountain" and he would rather give up than risk other people´s lives. On the other hand Cesare Maestri, who took part in this expedition, wrote the following thoughts in his diary: "Although I did everything in my power to succeed I know I have left something unfinished up there. I must return (to the Torre), I will return". His diary was eventually published in the book

"Arrampicare e il mio mestiere" (Climbing is my trade).

He kept his promise and returned, in the summer of 1958/59. With him was Toni Egger, who was considered the best Austrian climber at that moment. And they were joined here by Cesarino Fava and the Argentines A. and G. Daibagni and Juan P. Spikermann. This climb, like all the others, proved to be very difficult. Sometimes the snow was so hard that the spikes didn´t leave a scratch; but it could also be so soft that their boots sank ankle-deep.

Many times Maestri had the feeling that their life was worth nothing. They climbed very slowly and the weather became more and more threatening. "Toni goes ahead of us and manages to climb a wall so steep it is almost vertical. He climbs driving in one piton after another. Then I climb and leave the pitons in the wall. Then Toni screams: Cesare, the summit!"

"Exhaustion had dulled my senses, –wrote Maestri- I was a nervous wreck and I got ready to consummate the sacrifice to the most stupid of all human expressions: vanity".

Some of the thoughts he wrote in his diary are quite puzzling, considering that he achieved a goal he coveted and for which he willingly risked his life.

"I have struggled and lived for this moment. Was it worth it? Never have I understood so clearly that no mountain is worth a life. I loathe this summit. The wind, the pictures that were taken, the registered signatures, everything makes me sick! No. It wasn´t worth while."

Reading Maestri´s notes one has the impression that the literary side of his personality can be more convincing and disturbing than his self as a mountain climber.

The permanent risk of an avalanche made the descent very dangerous.

Suddenly a rock that broke away from the summit struck Toni Egger´s body and threw him down the precipice, while a terror-stricken Maestri helplessly looked on. A few meters from the base he himself fell off a slope. Luckily the snow was fresh and soft and cushioned the blow. He was found and rescued by Cesarino Fava. (Fava became quite a legend in Argentine mountaineering. During a rescue mission on the Aconcagua he got frostbite and lost both his feet and managed to walk on his stumps. Handicapped as he was he took part in several expeditions).

That climb must have been an ordeal for Maestri, not only because of all he went through but also because afterwards there were doubts as to his having reached the summit. Lacking all material proof of his accomplishment, with Toni

Egger´s disappearance he lost his only witness. Toni´s frozen body was found in 1975 on the Torre glacier but the camera was nowhere to be seen. Even though plenty of experienced climbers were willing to give him the benefit of the doubt, there were others – especially the English - who frankly didn´t believe his story.

These English mountaineers attempted to climb the Torre in 1967/68. With them went a group of four very experienced climbers and also the Argentine José Luis Fonrouge. There were differences of opinion about the tactics recommended by Fonrouge, and they finally resorted to the use of fixed ropes. Maybe that accounted for their failure in reaching the top in spite of their being very near. Bad weather only seemed to complicate even further this expedition which ended in frustration.

Meanwhile Cesare Maestri, severely wounded in his self-esteem, promised to return: "I will do things my way. I will return to the Torre and attack its most difficult wall in the most inconvenient season". In his mind, the issue had acquired an existentialist perspective: "...days will have vertical dimensions, made not of hours or minutes but only of centimeters and meters".

Nevertheless, whatever he did was under the close scrutiny of his critics. The disclosure of his intention of using a compressor to aid him in the ascent shocked traditional circles of mountain climbers that looked down with contempt on all kinds of mechanical climbing devices. This invention of his was most unusual. From the technological point of view, it was supposed to speed up the perforation process. The combination of bad weather conditions and fewer hours of daylight during the winter demanded greater speed in the fitting of pitons into the rock. Therefore, the use of a motor drill would meet these requirements and guarantee a quicker climbing rhythm as well. That was the good news. The bad news meant hoisting the gear with the sole use of his arms´ strength up the granite wall of the Torre, considering that the frame, motor and compressor weighed seventy kilos and the rest of the equipment –perforating pistols, air tubes, gas, spare parts, etc.- added an extra eighty or one hundred kilos more.

Consequently, if Maestri´s proposal shocked the purists it is also true that others admired his courage in daring to carry such an enormous weight up to the top.

He did actually manage to drive the piton into the rock "like a finger into butter", making "a beautiful, round hole with no rough edges".

However, brilliant as it was, his invention was not enough to guarantee success. Apart from the permanent storms and blizzards, they had other drawbacks –landslides that destroyed the shelter at the base, running out of provisions, among others- that finally forced them to give up the project. It was a downhearted Maestri who wrote: "No matter how hard I try to hold back my tears, I feel a sob knotting my throat. My feet·are cold and my clothes are torn...". They were only four hundred meters away from the top when they decided to give up their dream. They returned leaving the compressor hanging from the rock wall.

The Torre became his obsession. Three months later Maestri decided to give it another try. This time his efforts were rewarded: the weather was milder, he found the compressor there where he´d left it and it worked beautifully. He made good time and on the 2nd of December of 1970 he reached the summit. In Italy, there were tremendous expectations built around this climb. The media described Maestri´s conquest of the Torre as a milestone comparable to a feat in outer space.

Important financial concerns had sponsored the two expeditions. In his second book –"2000 meters of our life"- which he wrote together with his wife Fernanda, Maestri gives many details of the web of interests and human experiences behind the scenes of the climb, which stirs the curiosity of the public far beyond mountain climbing circles. Perhaps that induced Werner Herzog to film "Scream of Stone". The movie, which seems to suggest Maesri´s intense personal experience on the Torre, also offers a dazzling view of the mountains capable of capturing the attention of the public in general.

Usually Maestri is thought of as a skilled mountain climber, hence his nickname: "spider of the dolomites". However, he also became an original narrator who managed to endow mountaineering with all the attributes of a gripping novel not lacking in intrigue and passion.

In 1974 a team from Lecco guided by Casimiro Ferrari attempted to climb the Torre once again. Although Maestri had already shown the way to succeed, this team had chosen to follow the traditional procedures, that is with moderate means and a minimum of exhibitionism. The four that climbed up the west wall reached the top. They were Casimiro Ferrari himself, Mario Conti, Pino Negri and Daniele Chiappa. Apart from overcoming severe obstacles on the ice, they claimed to be the first to climb the ice "bonnet" capping the summit.

Silvia Metzeltin and Gino Buscaini, the well-informed and amusing authors of "Patagonia", give the following definition of the Torre: "It is a mischievous needle that wears its ice mushroom like a bonnet at an arrogant slant".

Should anyone ask an orthodox mountaineer who was the first to climb the Torre, the answer would invariably be Casimiro Ferrari. Although he never laid claim to having done so, the fact is that he not only treaded on the insolent bonnet, he was also seduced by the powerful landscape and settled there.

Lured by the victories of their Italian colleagues, mountain climbers of other countries decided to try their luck. In 1977 a team formed by three North Americans (Bragg, Carman and Milson) was the third to reach the top of the Torre. A fellow countryman, an eccentric and unpredictable character called Jim Bridwell, was also tempted to attack the Torre and entertained the idea of forming a team with the famous John Bachar and Mike Graham, whom he had met in Patagonia. However, the hurricanes and continuous snowstorms made the latter decide against the project, and Bridwell was forced to look for other partners. To his delight, an adventurer called Steve Brewer was quite willing to join him in the challenge and they both set off in what proved to be an unprecedented meteoric ascent.

Bridwell wrote: "I am aware that in only one day we have managed to climb higher than anyone else in the same lapse of time". He recounted that when he passed by Maestri´s compressor, which was by that time part of the mountain´s heritage, and leaving aside all purist prejudices: "...I was filled with admiration at the sight of this piece of machinery so close to this magnificent summit, and couldn´t help comparing the effort to carry it up to these heights with Hannibal´s crossing of the Alps".

In spite of the joy at having reached the top in record time, the weather threatened to become very nasty so they began a speedy descent. Inadvertently Bridwell had fastened round his body a rope that was frayed and it broke. He was violently launched into midair. Fortunately his reflexes were in top shape and he was able to catch on to an end of the rope. Although the accident lasted a very brief moment, he actually had time for some thoughts. He remembered asking himself questions, such as: "Will I get to see my little son when he´s born? Where does the rope end? I think I want to scream, but I say to myself: Shut up! Screaming won´t help me".

After having climbed the Torre in record time, and once he got over his moment of panic during the accident, Bridwell reached the following conclusion: "I am glad to think that if you´re not scared you don´t have fun. Because, if that is the case, then climbing the Torre is equivalent to spending two years in Disneyland".

According to the experts, 1986 was the year when the task that required great know-how and an outstanding capacity for making quick decisions was accomplished: the direct ascent on the east wall and the climb up the south side. It was a Yugoslav team that earned the credit of a climb that took them thirty-five days with only fourteen days of mild weather. Throughout the climb and at all times, they were exposed to the danger of falling blocks of ice.

Someone once wrote that: "...the direct route to the east wall had become the most difficult ascent in Patagonia, and therefore one of the most difficult in the whole world". And as regards the south wall: "...it is a vertical hell, permanently tortured by continuous volleys of pieces of ice that become detached from the top..."

The Yugoslavs were forced to endure one of the most violent storms ever registered on the Torre, to the point that it prevented them from making a halt to put on their snow jackets.

Silvo Karo, who was climbing with Franc Knez, was thrown into space by a violent gust of wind. He wrote: "Nothing could stop me from falling deeper and deeper into the void. Instinctively I tried to stop. Would Franc have been able to do it? How long would the ropes resist now that they were frayed after the climb?. Time seemed to have no end...but after a powerful jolt I realized it was all over: I was thirty meters below my partner". That was the happy outcome of this heroic exploit.

Silvia Metzeltin de Buscaini had rightfully predicted that the Torre would eventually attract all sorts of avid adventure seekers and daring mountaineers who loved the combination of risk and excitement. Among the many activities that could be considered medium-risk sports there is the case of a German, Matthis Pinn who practiced paragliding on the Torre. And we must mention the Argentine aviator Oscar Almirón who, in a display of originality, put down one of the skids of his helicopter on the ice bonnet crowning the summit.

We therefore reach the conclusion that the mythical Torre considered by many as "the most difficult mountain in the world" became, over the years, the adequate environment for bold, audacious men and women with a strong desire for risk combined with fantasy, and adventure with a touch of glory.

The Hielo Patagónico, the historiography of the Fitz Roy and the Torre became known to the world after the incursion of "The Spiders of Lecco" in the Patagonian Andes.

Lecco, situated on the eastern branch of the Como Lake, is the gateway to the Alps. It was, and still is a famous center of renowned mountain climbers. Its fame is due to the international exploits carried out by the members of the group called "Spiders of Lecco", which was founded in 1946 by the legendary climber Ricardo Cassin. The history of this group in Patagonia began in 1955, in an expedition which was organized by a priest, Father Alberto María De Agostini, that reached the summit of Monte Sarmiento. Carlo Mauri, from Lecco, was a member of the team. During the trip Mauri heard talk about a "granite needle" that was invulnerable. Word got around in no time, and the very next year there were two Italian expeditions gathered at the base of the Torre.

One of them (Italian/Argentine) was formed by Folco Doro, Walter Bonatti and Mauri himself. The other group was headed by the famous climber Bruno de Tassis and one of its members was Cesare Maestri, "the Spider of the Dolomites".

That marked the beginning of an ongoing relationship between the mountains of the Hielo Patagónico and Italian climbers.

In the 70´s, another group from Lecco attempted to climb the Torre. It was led by Mauri and counted among its members several top mountaineers like Casimiro Ferrari, Roberto Chiappa and Folco Doro. Unfortunately, bad weather and technical difficulties they found on the ice wall forced them to return when they were barely two hundred meters away from the top. This was Mauri´s second attempt. His first ascent had been in 1958 and also had a disappointing outcome. However, Mauri was not the typical mountaineer who evaluated an expedition in terms of success/failure depending on whether or not he reached the summit. He carried out every expedition not only as a mountain climber but also as an explorer and historical researcher. He documented his experience like a journalist or a photographer.

He was one of the "seven men" who took part in the Ra Expeditions that were organized by the Norwegian Thor Heyerdahl on board the Kon Tiki (a raft made of papyri). The purpose of those expeditions was to find out if a raft made of that material could possibly have sailed the ocean and if the people of Ancient Egypt had arrived at some American beach before becoming "sculptors, pharaohs and mummies". Despite the general skepticism generated by the project, Thor obstinately accomplished it in the company of his bold team mates who represented seven different nations: the Italian Carlo Mauri, photographer; the Mexican Santiago Genovés, boatswain; the North American Norman Baker, navigator; the Egyptian George Sourial, deep-sea diver; the Russian Yuri

Senkevitch, physician, and the African from Chad, Abdullah Djibrine, an expert on papyrus. Thor reached the conclusion that "...a vessel built with papyri can sail in the sea", and that the Atlantic Ocean may well have been, in the past, a route towards the West.

Mauri was undoubtedly a man of great personality, an explorer with an inquiring mind. We can easily assume that he felt a great attraction for the Andes, and that his incursions into the Cordillera were motivated by an interest and projects that went far beyond his experience as a mountaineer. He was a keen, tireless traveler who was full of ambitious plans. But his health gave way. He had a heart condition which caused his death, in 1982.

After two failed attempts he solemnly promised he would return to the Torre. Unfortunately he was unable to fulfill what had been one of his greatest dreams.

Like Mauri, Casimiro Ferrari was another firm admirer of the "Patagonian wonders". He even settled in that region and became a Patagonian inhabitant. He was always a winner. Both in mountain climbing and in his experiences traveling through Patagonian land, he never knew failure or frustration. Maybe that was partly due to his persevering nature and the capacity to always have his own way. On the Hielo Continental he repeatedly attacked the Murallón, also nicknamed the "bewitched mountain". Twice during 1980 he was forced to abandon on account of the persistent bad weather and violent wind. The Murallón is a huge, 2831-meters-high stone block, and was considered by the Lecco team one of the most challenging peaks.

Ferrari wasn't one to take no for an answer, so he insisted again in December/January of 1982/83. Once more, bad weather forced him to give up. The following year he decided to give it another try. By now he was feeling quite angry with the Murallón, but he was definitely not going to be defeated by this, or any, mountain. On this opportunity he went with several members of the "Spiders of Lecco" group, but even that was not sufficient to triumph against the elements. Dejectedly they began their return over the Upsala glacier, each one finding it very hard to assimilate this defeat. Then, very unexpectedly the weather improved. Unhesitatingly, Ferrari went back to the Murallón with two of his mates, Alde and Vitali (the other four had already left); this time he was determined to win.

On the 10th of February they reached the summit by the northeast crest.

Ferrari once again put on a brilliant performance in 1987, when he reached the summit of the Risso Patrón peak. Not only was he the first to climb that mountain, he also carried out –in winter- the inaugural west/east crossing of the Hielo Continental from the Falcon Fiord to the estancia Cristina.

In 1994 he climbed up the Mermoz needle, thus repeating the feat that had first been accomplished in 1974 by the Argentines Fermín Olaechea, Guillermo Vieiro and Héctor Cuiñas.

The "Patagonian" Casimiro Ferrari in a way made up for Andreas Madsen´s grief. Madsen was quite content to live in awe of his beloved mountains and felt offended by the mountain climbers who he considered intruders in his world of worship. Whereas Ferrari, who was equally seduced by these mountains and their magic, dared to explore them, to become acquainted with them. Metaphorically speaking, they became his comrades.

Casimiro´s wife once asked him:

"Who do you love more, your family or the mountains of Patagonia?"

Both" –he answered-. Later, he admitted: "I was wrong. Finally the mountains won. So much so that my wife promptly demanded a divorce. I sold the wire factory I had in Lecco. I left behind my parents, three brothers and two grownup sons in Ballabio, Como. And in 1996 I settled here in Punta Lago, next to the Viedma glacier, with some remorse but without sorrow".

Ferrari, like Madsen, fulfilled an old dream, which was to find the meaning of life in a space with no boundaries and to live in absolute freedom. "With work I can live... but *andinism* and Patagonia make me feel alive".

With the money he would have needed to buy an apartment in Milan he bought an estancia of 26,000 hectares plus sheep, cows, horses, guanacos, hens and turkeys. Whenever mountaineers came to his place he offered his hospitality and promoted agri-tourism. All that gave him much more personal pleasure than financial profit. This was his explanation: "It is a way of making my friends from Lecco –and other not such close friends- get to love this place. Patagonia and its mountains mean everything to me: here I found physical and spiritual freedom".

He was eternally grateful to Mauri for having aroused his interest in Patagonia, ever since that trip they made together in 1965. It was in his memory that he built the shelter "Carlo Mauri" on the spot where he camped the first time he explored the Andean mountains.

The first pioneers who settled in the Andes have been dead decades ago. They would surely be surprised to know that in many points their views coincided with those of the mountaineers who once dared trespass on the sacred ground of their beloved mountains. The genuine mountaineer doesn´t care for the outbreak of mountain tourism that belittles the greatness of the Patagonian Andes and lowers the standards of professional performance.

Andinism became a fashionable sport and, as such, it is looked down upon by the true *andinists* with as much contempt as was shown to them by the proud pioneers of the past.

One day, in the middle of a ruthless winter, Casimiro Ferrari suddenly fell ill and was urgently taken to Calafate for proper medical attention. This man, who had triumphed over the most challenging peaks, was unable to overcome his physical ailments. He died in August of 2001.

It was unfair. "Casimiro the Patagonian" shouldn´t have been deprived so soon of that daily, wonderful view of the Torre and the Fitz Roy, those beloved mountains that filled his life with meaning.

After all, he had left everything behind just to be able to commune every day with the Patagonian Andes.

20.- A LAND OF LEGEND

The first to set eyes on this polar area–calculated at around 20,000 km2 –
was Juan Fernández Ladrillero, a Spanish navigator and explorer who was trying
to cross the Strait from the Pacific to the Atlantic in a voyage of reconnaissance.
That was in 1557. Up to that moment all the crossings had been the other way
round, that is from the Atlantic Ocean to the Pacific. His ship, the *"San Luis"*,
was blown by a storm away from the rest of the fleet he commanded, and entered
a deep fiord. A fascinating landscape appeared before him: a vast expanse of ice
with an imposing landscape of snow-covered mountains. Centuries later that
fiord was called Eyre.

Ladrillero made three more voyages to that region, which he christened
"Sierra Nevada". Many years later the initial name was substituted by Hielo
Continental Sur.

There were other subsequent explorations whose reports have been very
valuable in establishing the particular characteristics of that polar area.

It was only in 1914 that the first expedition that had the specific purpose of
crossing the Hielo Continental was carried out. Its name was "Flora Argentina"
and was formed by the botanist and geologist of the La Plata Museum Cristóbal
M. Hicken; the naturalist Rodolfo Hauthal; the chemist and naturalist Federico
Reichert and the painter/photographer Hans Jorgensen. The Flora Argentina
Committee, which was created in 1911, sponsored that research voyage that
tried to reach the Pacific crossing the Hielo Continental.

After sailing in waters of the Argentino Lake, they camped in the vicinity of
the Los Témpanos canal, near the corrie discovered by Perito Moreno.

Reichert described it as: "A land of legend, beautiful beyond compare. The
huge ice wall stood before us. It was a fascinating, alluring picture and I doubt
that there are many places on earth where snow and ice commune so intimately
with the vegetation layer as in Southern Patagonia".

Reichert had traveled widely around the world and was particularly attracted
to mountain landscapes. Although he had climbed peaks in the Alps and the

Caucasus, none had managed to arouse his interest as the Andes. He developed a passion for everything connected with the Andean range, which he explored with a scientist´s thoroughness.

In 1904 Wenceslao Escalante, Argentine Minister of Agriculture, asked Rodolfo Hauthal –geologist of the La Plata Museum- to appoint foreign scientists and technicians. Among them was Fritz Reichert, who was later naturalized. After his arrival in 1904 he took part in an exploration to the Northern Puna; the following year, with the researcher Roberto Hebling, he went on an expedition to the areas of Tupungato and the Aconcagua, in the part of the cordillera situated in the province of Mendoza.

Cristóbal M.Hicken had carried out botanical research in different regions of Argentina; his specific objective was to study the characteristics and formations of the local flora.

The expedition Flora Argentina reached the inter-oceanic water-shed, which is the point where waters of the two oceans divide. Reichert describes it as "a remarkably wild place...the traveler can´t help feeling shaken at the awesome view of this world of everlasting ice".

The naturalist Rodolfo Hauthal –he was German-born and later a naturalized Argentine- was a professor of Geology and Botany at the La Plata University. He was the first to explore the Moreno glacier, regarding which he wrote: "I cannot find the words to express what goes through my mind like a sheer sensation, like a direct feeling of what is godlike and eternal, of infinity".

The surveys of the glaciers and the geographical studies carried out by the expedition in 1914 provided a thorough and detailed knowledge of that polar section of the cordillera.

The first flight over the extreme south of Patagonia was performed by the French aviator Omar Page, in 1914. It was in Punta Arenas, Ushuaia, flying over Cape Horn.

In 1916 another important expedition took place. It was sponsored by the German Scientific Society of Buenos Aires and the objective was to explore the central area of the Hielo Continental. Among the members of the group were the geologist Lutz Wittle; a Swiss-Argentine chemist called Alfredo Koelliker, and Hans Jorgensen; also two qualified assistants: T. Silbermany and F. Diener. In the course of this exploration they discovered the mountain chain Mariano Moreno and they determined the point where the waters divide, which was west of the Fitz Roy. With all these new studies of an up to then unexplored region it was possible to determine that the Hielo Continental covers an area approximately 400 kilometers long that is formed by intertwined plateaus, with very impressive glaciers descending to the east and to the west.

On their return, Wittle expressed: "We were very sorry to leave such a beautiful place". And this is what Koelliker wrote in an exalted prose about Patagonia: " You are the idol of freedom and greatness, as yet far from surrendering to the yoke of a degenerate civilization. You are the land of strong men and a free spirit".

In 1916 two Chilean pilots, Fuentes and Castro, on board an 80 hp Bleriot, carried out the first flight over the Magellan Strait, in 23 minutes.

In 1921 Mario Pozzatti, who was a pilot of the AeroClub of Punta Arenas, inaugurated the first postal flight in that region, carrying a mailbag from Punta Arenas to Río Gallegos.

In 1928 Gunther Plüschow made the first postal flight between Punta Arenas and Ushuaia. Shortly after he flew over the Hielo Continental with his hydroplane D-1313, accompanied by the copilot Ernst Dreblow. Plüschow was the first to make exploratory flights and his incursions produced very valuable information.

He wrote: "Wherever I go, I only see ice, ice and more ice. Anyone would think I was back in the Ice Age! Everything has become one unique and continuous bar of sparkling ice that fills and covers all...".

Plüschow arrived in Patagonia on board his schooner "Feuerland" (Tierra del Fuego), after fighting for his country in the First World War and having proven his expertise as a pilot. On his ship he carried all the parts of a Heinkel D-24 hydroplane, which he named "Cóndor de Plata". In 1931, during a flight over the Argentino Lake, a cable of the rudder cut, and the plane fell from a six-hundred-meter-height into the lake. Although Plüschow and Dreblow had time to jump neither of their parachutes opened, and they both died.

A mountain peak near San Martín Lake bears his name.

Many other peaks have been named in memory of aviators who were seduced by Patagonia. Such is the case of the French Saint Exupéry, Guillaumet and Jean Mermoz. Another renowned pilot, the Argentine Oscar Almirón, flew over the region for more than twenty years with a helicopter, and managed to save the life of explorers and *andinists* who had lost their way and would have surely died had it not been for his timely rescue.

Years later, only flights destined to rescue people were allowed. That was decided by the authorities as a way of protecting the natural environment.

In 1931, the Salesian priest Father Alberto María de Agostini, together with the geologist Egidio Feruglio, crossed the glacier westwards until they reached the summit of Monte Torino, from where they sighted the Pacific Ocean.

In 1933 Federico Reichert took part in an expedition that left San Martín Lake bound for the Pacific Ocean, and returned to the ice region. A member of the group was the first woman to set foot on the Hielo Continental, the researcher Ilse von Rentzell. When the team reached the dividing line of the Hielo Continental they discovered the Lautaro, an active volcano of approximately 3.000 meters´ height.

These two last expeditions marked the end of the romantic or pioneer period.

In 1937 the Dirección General de Parques Nacionales de Argentina (National Parks Department of Argentina) created the Los Glaciares National Park.

Between 1944 and 1945 the US Air Force, appointed by the Chilean Government, carried out an aero-photographic survey of the glacier region, thus completing the information of its geology and geography.

There was an expedition to the Hielo Patagónico in 1952. The team was commanded by Emiliano Huerta. Among its members were Mario Bertone,Folco Doro, Arigo Bianchi and A.Ruiz Beramendi. From Lake Viedma, they walked across a long extension from North to South, and covered two hundred kilometers in nineteen days. One afternoon, once the fog had cleared, they viewed the Exmouth Fiord and the forests surrounding it. Huerta wrote: "We almost fell on our knees at the sight of that radiant vision; our lips murmured a silent prayer of thanks to God. With feverish excitement we watched the waters beat on the coast, and countless cascades covered by forests of beech trees. Oh, heavens! That scene was like a part of paradise. After so many days of trudging and living on ice, with all its beautiful but terrible whiteness, that was equivalent to warmth and well-being".

During the journey they were able to pinpoint the mountain Lautaro, which was none other than the volcano that was first seen by Reichert and that others had ineffectively tried to locate.

This expedition was a deciding factor in the creation of the National Institute of the Hielo Continental Patagónico, under the command of Emiliano Huerta. Over the years, the Institute organized several other expeditions.

At the beginning of 1956 Harold W.Tilman, -a British explorer, yachtsman and mountain climber- with the sponsorship of the Royal Geographical Society, made the first crossing of the Hielo from the West, from Calvo Fiord; he climbed the Calvo corrie until the blizzard forced him to cross the Cordillera and then down the Moreno Glacier on the edge of the Argentino Lake.

In 1960 Eric Shipton, an Englishman who was at the time Vice-president of the National Geographic Society, led an important expedition which made the first North-South crossing of the Hielo, from the Jorge Montt glacier to the vast Upsala glacier, and ended in the estancia La Cristina, on Lago Argentino. It was a carefully planned expedition and adequately equipped to deal with the challenge of crossing the northern region of the Hielo Continental Sur which had been, up to that moment, unexplored.

The first landing on the Hielo was in 1962, on the Upsala glacier. It was performed by the pilot Mario Olezza on board a DC3 of the Argentine Air Force.

In 1969 two groups of Japanese mountain climbers entered the Hielo following different itineraries. They became renowned for having chosen the riskiest routes to climb the most challenging peaks all over the world, and registered several fatal accidents. One of the teams was led by Chotoro Nakasima, of the University of Kioto; they explored different regions with research purposes. The other group, which was organized by the Rokko Gakuin Alpine Club, attempted a West-east journey from the Exmouth fiord to the Upsala glacier. They had to put up with awful weather. They had skis and sleds and carried approximately 600 kilos in supplies and equipment.

By that time all expeditions were equipped with first-class gear, high technology instruments for every possible contingency and efficient aerial and naval support.

Expeditions from different countries became more and more frequent: Argentina, Japan, New Zealand, Italy, France, Germany, Austria, etc.

In the 80´s a French group carried out a real prowess and crossed the "ice fields" from South to North. They were Jean Louis Hourcadette, Bernard Doligez, Roger Hemon and Marc Roquefere. They advanced between the Ultima Esperanza fiord and the Tyndall glacier over regions that had never been explored before. They marched with sleds and skis through impossible places like the crevices of the Balmaceda glacier and always beaten by blizzards and snowstorms to the limit of their endurance

21.- A CONTROVERSIAL JOURNEY

As in the case of Cesare Maestri´s ascent of the Torre and the controversy as to whether he had or not reached the summit, in 1985 it was Giuliano Giongo who aroused serious doubts regarding his attack on the Hielo Continental. He was a renowned mountaineer with a solid record both in the Alps and in Patagonia, where he climbed the Torre Egger -following a new route- and also the Fitz Roy.

In this case, Giongo´s intention was to cross the Hielo Continental lengthwise, alone and in winter.

He maintained he had accomplished his purpose, and yet he wasn´t able to produce convincing proof. He hesitated and lacked precision; he stressed all that could be sensationalist but refrained from expressing a technical evaluation. All those who had previous experience in penetrating the Hielo doubted him, especially the famous and conscientious climber Walter Bonatti.

This was Giuliano Giongo´s story:

He advanced through Paso Marçoni carrying 35 kilos in equipment and supplies. His tent was very light, similar to a bivouac bag with a mouthpiece that would allow him to breathe in the face of an emergency or in case he should be covered by snow. He said: "On the 13th of July I leave on foot and I can finally count on my own and sole resources. I bivouac in old huts that the wind has destroyed, or under a rock; I overcome vertical ice cascades crossing the cordillera, until I enter Chile... Very strong wind coming from the South propelled me through Hickem Pass and on the 21st of July I reach my destination at the height of Los Mellizos".

From there Giuliano Giongo reversed his itinerary and went southwards. The blizzards were almost intolerable. He continues: "I still haven´t had time to lie down and I´m again submerged in the storm. Snow melts when it touches the garment my body has heated, and that is the base on which more snow will accumulate. Half an hour later I must use the mouthpiece to breathe because my tent-bag is completely covered by snow and it has become so heavy that my legs are trapped by its weight. It is only through the mouthpiece that I feel the hell about to be unleashed. Every night I prepare a cellophane bag with snow and leave it beside me. At dawn I put it inside my eiderdown. Thanks to the body heat, within two hours it will turn into a kind of watery mud which allows me to cook using much less gas... When I leave my den and come out into the open I wonder how can one possibly spend the night in these conditions".

Still, he advanced. He went through the Cinco Glaciares Pass and approached the Italia plateau. On the 4th of August he reached the Andrew fiord, which was a place of difficult access that no one had entered up to that moment. He fought against that difficult surface for one whole week and finally reached the Polonia plateau.

Ten days later he fell into a deep crevice and was forced to remain there because of a storm; during those three days he managed to survive thanks to the careful rationing of the food he carried in his pocket. He was tied to a rope attached to the sled which was firm because the ice had welded the skids to the ground. Giongo was actually able to ascend because the sled supported his weight without detaching itself from the surface of the glacier.

There were still ten more days to go but he finally made it. He was utterly exhausted when he got to the estancia "La Cristina".

And the discussion began.

Walter Bonatti was a man of firm principles who believed that prowess in mountaineering must be easily proven. He had serious doubts about Giongo's expedition. Although Giongo defended himself as best he could he wasn´t actually able to produce solid proof to back his story. Others expressed their views about this journey that he carried out in winter in a most desolate and implacable territory, as a suicidal act of heroism. Other experts described his feat as a partial North-South journey carried out by Giuliano Longo on his own, with skis and sled; he "entered by Marconi Pass and reached the estancia Cristina".

Things have changed over the years and nowadays there is quite an active traffic on the Hielo Continental: special vehicles can cross it during the winter season, when the snow levels the crevices, and planes and helicopters can take off and land. There is excellent cartography available, and satellite tracking provides all the necessary information.

In spite of modern technology, the ice fields still attract explorers and mountaineers from all over the world who want to conquer a part of the Andean range and obtain their share of glory and success. Nature is still wild and implacable: the violent storms and raging winds that blow at 150 or 200 kph constantly drive human resistance to its very limit, and that alone is enough to pique the curiosity and pride of recalcitrant mountain climbers.

There are still many peaks and places that have hardly been explored and are therefore considered an exciting challenge for all those who are "possessed" by a dauntless need of adventure, and who are urged to try new itineraries and routes across this impressive white territory.

A land of ice and snow, forever isolated and condemned to the lashing of a violent, ruthless wind.

REFERENCES

AZARA, Félix de, *Viajes por la América Meridional* (Espasa Calpe)

BARROS, Alvaro, *Indios, fronteras y seguridad interior* (Hachette)

BERTONE, Mario, *Aspectos Glaciológicos del Hielo Continental Patagónico* (El Ateneo)

BIEDMA, José Juan, *Crónica histórica del Nahuel Huapi* (Emecé)

CALDCLEUG, Alejandro, *Viaje a Chile* (Editorial del Pacífico)

CALVO, Mayo, *Secretos y tradiciones Mapuches* (Editorial Andrés Bello)

CRAWFORD, R., *A través de la Pampa y de los Andes* (Eudeba)

DE AGOSTINI, Alberto M., S.S, *Andes Patagónicos. Viajes de Exploración a la Cordillera Patagónica Austral* (Kraft)

FINO, J. Frederic, *Andinismo en la Argentina* (Club Andino Bariloche)

GUEVARA, Tomás, *Psicología del pueblo araucano* (Imprenta Cervantes)

HAIGH, Samuel, *Viaje a Chile en la época de la Independencia* (Editorial del Pacífico)

HALVORSEN, Patricia, *Entre el río de las Vueltas y los hielos continentales* (Vinciguerra)

HEAD, F. B, *Las pampas y los Andes* (Hyspamérica)

HOSNE, Roberto, *Barridos por el Viento, Historias de la Patagonia desconocida* (Planeta) *Patagonia, Leyenda y realidad* (Eudeba)

MADSEN, Andreas, *La Patagonia vieja* (Galerna)

MIERS, John, *Viajes por Chile y El Plata* (Solar)

MORENO, Francisco P., *Viaje a la Patagonia Austral* (Solar – Hachette)

ONELLI, Clemente, *Trepando los Andes* (Marymar)

OSTROWSKI, Víctor, *Más alto que los cóndores* (Albatros)

PALESE DE TORRES, A, *Expedición al Aconcagua* (Ediciones Geográficas Argentina)

PASQUALI, Patricia, *San Martín* (Planeta)

PECHMANN, Guillermo, *El Campamento 1878* (Eudeba)

PRIETO, Adolfo, *Los Viajeros ingleses y la emergencia de la literatura argentina* (Sudamericana)

PROCTOR, R, *Narraciones del viaje por la Cordillera de los Andes* (La Cultura Argentina)

RAS, Norberto, *Crónicas de la Frontera Sur* (Hemisferio Sur)

SCHMIDTMEYER, Peter, *Viaje a Chile* (Claridad)

SEKELJ, Tibor, *Tempestad sobre el Aconcagua* (Albatros)

SOLIS, Leonardo León, *Maloqueros araucanos en las fronteras*

TSCHIFFELY, Aimé F., *Por este camino hacia el Sur. Un viaje por la Patagonia y Tierra del Fuego* (El Jagüel)

VALLARD, Johan A., *El hombre y los Andes (*Ediciones Culturales)
YGOBONE, Aquiles, *Viajeros científicos de la Patagonia (*Galerna)

PHOTOGRAPHS

Archivo General de la Nación
Ediciones de Andinismo de la revista SWING
Revista CONTINENTE (varios números)
Revista PANORAMA y SIETE DIAS, Editorial Abril
ARGENTINA AUSTRAL,Tomo III
Revista IMAGEN
Revista SPORT ILUSTRADO
Cuadernos Patagónicos TECHINT

This second edition published January 2006,
Printed in Argentina by Gráfica DELING
with 1.500 copies.